D0772384

Longhorn Justice

Cattle baron Nat Erdlatter has built his empire by taking what he wants then ruthlessly holding on to it. Even now, with the Homestead Act encouraging people to settle on range land that he has always considered his own, he believes that his needs take preference over the government's decrees.

But times are changing and the citizens of the nearby town of Enterprise are angered by his latest callous act, none more so than his former ranch hands Clem Rawlings and Gus Farley, who become embroiled in an affair which can only lead to violence, and danger. . . .

Longhorn Justice

Will DuRey

A Black Horse Western

ROBERT HALE · LONDON

ISBN 978-0-7198-1236-1

Robert Hale Limited
Clerkenwell House
Clerkenwell Green
London EC1R 0HT

www.halebooks.com

Typeset by
Derek Doyle & Associates, Shaw Heath
Printed and bound in Great Britain by
CPI Antony Rowe, Chippenham and Eastbourne

CHAPTER ONE

Dusk, and although the sky overhead has drained to a dull ash-tree grey, great swags of colour: pink, orange and yellow, illuminate the western horizon. On a ridge, silhouetted against the spectacle of the sun's farewell, a lone rider sits his steed. The horse rears, its forehoofs clawing high in the air and its full mane and tail flare out like battle-tattered banners. The rider removes his hat and with great sweeps of his arm uses it to signal his position to those on the plain below, then he disappears over the far side of the ridge.

The extravagance of Vinny Erdlatter's gesture is typical of the young man's mannerisms and on another occasion might arouse a scornful comment from among those who witness it, but on this night it excites nothing more than a wry grin from the back rider because the eldest member of the group is Vinny's father, their boss. Nat Erdlatter raises his right hand, an order to halt for those riding with him. If he is surprised by his son's appearance or has an explanation for the beckoning gesture, he does not disclose it to those who ride with him and they know that he will not welcome their views on the matter. So they wait in silence until he issues his next command.

Nat Erdlatter is a man who trusts only his own instincts and acts accordingly. He is a man of pride who acknowledges neither pleasure nor pain; he is a survivor who lives each day as though he is sitting in a high-stakes poker game; a demonstration of emotion, he believes, is a display of weakness upon which an enemy will pounce. Over the years he has been forced to confront many enemies. Now, he is a self-made cattle baron with stock grazing over a vast portion of Wyoming territory and, with his customary cunning, willpower and merciless adherence to the creed that his needs alone are paramount, he intends to rule the area for many more years. He hasn't survived seasons of drought and winters of bitter cruelty, range wars and Indian attacks just to allow someone else to grow rich. He is Nat Erdlatter and is prepared to kill anyone who threatens his authority.

Nat taps his spurs against the flanks of his big chestnut gelding and leads the three other riders up and over the ridge in pursuit of his son. Vinny has merged into another bunch of riders gathered under a widespread cottonwood. They are five in number and they wait with unnatural stillness as the new arrivals approach. From fifty yards a rope can be observed that has been slung over one of the tree's lower branches, the noose at the end has been tightened around the neck of one of the horsemen, stretching him so that he is standing in his stirrups, his head held awkwardly high, desperately seeking an angle that will keep his air passage open. His hands are fastened behind his back and the fear that is etched on his face becomes increasingly evident as Nat and his men slither their mounts to a halt.

'They caught him, Pa.' Vinny is trying to restrain his excitement but his voice is higher and louder than normal. He points a little way down the slope. A small fire burns, the light smoke drifts languidly away across the meadow-land. 'He was putting an iron on our beef. Red and the boys caught him.' He turns to one of the other men for confirmation.

'That's right, Mr Erdlatter.' The speaker is Jos 'Red' Hammond, foreman of Erdlatter's spread. He is a gruff man in coarse clothes that are dirty and dust-covered, and his stubbled, scarred face and unkempt hair are no less dirty. It is the colour of his hair, a bright ginger, which has given rise to the sobriquet by which he is known throughout the territory. 'About to over-brand some steers. We were going to string him up. Figured that would be what you'd want us to do.'

'Stealing cattle.' Nat Erdlatter speaks to the bound man astride a pinto pony, his voice unraised, the words unhurried, the very blandness of the delivery making his pronouncement more chilling to the listener. 'Only one punishment for that.'

The prisoner's eyes are enormous, enlarged by fear and his desperate battle to breathe. He tries to speak but Grat Todd tugs at the rope causing the rough circlet around his neck to tighten. To those watching it seems that his neck stretches another inch, as though he will be choked to death while still astride his pony, a possibility made all the more likely by the gasping, gargling sounds that escape from his mouth.

One of the three who followed Nat Erdlatter to this point urges his horse alongside that of his employer. Clem Rawlings has been working cattle on Erdlatter's Circle-E for a year. 'That's Pat Baker,' he declares, his voice betraying his distaste for what is about to happen.

The inference of criticism in Clem's interruption doesn't please Nat Erdlatter. 'Not interested in his name. We hang cattle-thieves.'

'There must be a mistake,' Clem says. 'Pat works for Harv Golden. They've got a place along the Westwater.'

Nat Erdlatter turns angrily. 'Nester,' he says, the word spat out as though it is fetid fish. 'Stealing is what you expect from those people.'

Clem has heard all the stories that are told about Nat Erdlatter's early years in Wyoming and knows that they abound in gunfights with land-grabbers and the lynching of rustlers. Some of the stories he is prepared to believe are true, but here and now he finds it hard to believe that they are gathered around this cottonwood to hang Pat Baker. Pat is about his own age and if they meet in Enterprise they nod an acknowledgement of each other, but they aren't friends. They had once had a drink together in Jake Clewson's saloon but that had been a mistake. Clem had been new in town and had bought himself a beer at the first bar he'd come to. Pat had struck up a conversation with him on the assumption that he was working on one of the farms north of town, because the cattlemen always used the Diamond or the Prairie Paradise.

When the truth of the situation was revealed they kept apart; nothing personal at that time, just both conscious of the fact that their employment virtually depended on maintaining the show of disrespect that nesters had for ranchers and vice versa. But that show isn't the cause of the coldness that has developed between Clem and Pat, there is a different reason for that altogether.

Even so, Clem speaks again. 'Ain't likely that Pat would steal your cattle, Mr Erdlatter.' His words win a scowl from the old man and a glance or two of derision from some of the others gathered there. No one offers to support his attempted defence.

Pat Baker is making a final effort to speak. The farm worker's eyes settle on the young cowboy, his breathing is nothing more than a ragged series of gasps, gurgles and sobs. It is difficult for Clem to know if Pat recognizes him, all he knows for sure is that the look he has fixed on him is a plea for help. Clem scans the meadow-land, seeking anything he can offer to mitigate Pat's crime. There is only the small fire and the smoke dissipating into the gloom of the approaching night. Nothing else.

He is about to speak, about to voice a thought that needs to be heard, but as he opens his mouth his horse is nudged to the left and old Gus Farley edges forward, coming between Clem and Nat Erdlatter. Gus, semi-slouched in the saddle as is his style, holds Clem's gaze, offering a warning not to rile the boss again, not if he hopes to continue working at the Circle-E. Gus has

9

worked for Nat Erdlatter for many years, knows the signs when the boss man's temper is on a short fuse and nothing ignites his dynamite more swiftly than arguments from someone whose time he is paying for.

Then it happens, while Clem's attention is diverted by Gus's manoeuvre, old man Erdlatter mutters, 'Get it done,' then turns his horse and heads back over the ridge to continue his homeward journey, the lynching worth no more consideration than any of the other ruthless decisions he has taken since coming to this territory.

Vinny yips, loud and sudden, like he's driving strays back to the herd, and the hat which is once more in his hand, is swatted against the pinto's rump. The little horse bounds forward a handful of strides but, obedient to its training, stops when it realizes there is no weight on its back, no pressure nor prick of command on its flanks. Behind it the branch creaks as it bends to the downward pull of Pat Baker's swinging, kicking body.

For a moment every mounted man is still, watching the farmer's vain struggle. His body turns and for a moment, probably the last of his life, his eyes meet those of Clem Rawlings. They are wide, imploring, not seeking release from the noose but demanding some last request of the man with whom he'd once drunk a beer. Then his body jerks and the riders watch in silence until his kicking ceases and his suspended body swings slightly and turns in an ever shortening arc.

Vinny is the first to speak, jerking his horse first towards those who had caught Pat Baker then back to where Clem, Gus and Slippy Anderson watch. His back straightens and his shoulders are back, looking like one of the statues back East that have been erected to celebrate the gallant deeds of Civil War generals.

'That's how the Circle-E deals with rustlers,' he declares, convincing more than one of those within earshot that he believes he has taken a step in emulation of his father's actions.

Clem nudges his horse's flanks, moves it away from the hanging tree and wanders down to the dying fire. There are a few hot ashes, here and there a spark. He steps down and stamps them into extinction, his mind filled with thoughts of Pat Baker. He'd seen him earlier that evening, riding south, heading as he so often did for the Yates spread. Or had he been wrong in that assumption. Had his assessment of Pat's character been a mistake? Had Pat been dabbling in rustling? He shook his head. Perhaps he and Pat hadn't been friends but he didn't think he could be so far wrong about a man. He climbs back on to his saddle and rejoins the group under the tree.

Vinny is making the most noise, boasting about the authority of the Erdlatters and the Circle-E but being careful not to look at the now ugly face of the hanging man. Someone, either Carl Pelton or Tiny Duggett, has scrawled the word Rustler on a scrap of paper and used a nail to attach it to Pat's shirt. They are encouraging Vinny's bravado and talking about riding into Enterprise for a celebratory drink but Red Hammond squashes that plan with details of the work he has lined up for them in the morning.

11

'It means an early start,' he warns them, 'so let us get back to the bunkhouse.'

Clem rounds up the pinto and leads the way back to the Circle-E.

CHAPTER TWO

Neither the callous attitude of old man Erdlatter nor the puffed-up pleasure that the lynching has given his son sit easily with Clem Rawlings. He sits alone, refusing to sit in a penny-a-point card game and steps outside when the unexpected return of Dusty Thoms and Rollo Wilson from the east boundary line camp evokes a cruel account of the prairie lynching.

While it is yet more than an hour until dawn, Clem hasn't slept and knows he will not sleep this night. He leaves the seven other men in the bunkhouse to their dreams, saddles his own working pony and Pat Baker's pinto, and rides clear of the Circle-E. He is aware that what he plans to do will anger the boss of the Circle-E but no alternative course of action occurs to him. Whatever Pat Baker might or might not have done, it seems to Clem that the lynching was unnecessary and that leaving him hanging from the tree as a symbol of Nat Erdlatter's power will be sickeningly offensive to those who knew and liked the young man.

Clem's initial attempt to lower Pat's body on to the

pinto is nullified by the horse. It refuses to be backed under the dangling form of its former rider, shying away like a maiden being presented as a bride to a diseased old man. Eventually he is forced to cut the rope and the body falls to the ground. It takes all Clem's strength to lift the dead weight on to the skittish horse. He covers the body with a sheet of canvas before tying it securely to the animal for the journey ahead.

Turning his back to the hint of light in the east, Clem rides off at a steady canter, setting a course which will both avoid the town of Enterprise and stay well clear of the approaches to the Circle-E. He doesn't want to be intercepted by any of Nat Erdlatter's crew until he's delivered Pat Baker's body to Harv Golden. Harv Golden and his wife settled in the area little more than two years ago and their farm is sited along the Westwater, up towards the border with Montana. With luck, Clem will have returned Pat's body to Harv Golden and be back at the Circle-E before Charlie Sow, the cook, has cleared away breakfast.

To the best of Clem's knowledge, Pat Baker was the only extra hand employed by Harv, and the farm itself is unknown territory to the Circle-E cowboy. He has no way of knowing where Pat slept at night, nor if the Goldens are aware that their hired help hasn't made it back to the farm. Consequently, when he reaches the property, he sits for a moment to study the layout before hailing the house.

The living place itself is little more than a soddy with the addition of some stout wooden supports which bestow upon it a sort of permanency that many of the other settler homes lack. Off to the left of the house is a timber barn, a building of sturdier construction than the low building in which the Goldens live. There is nothing visible to the eye or audible to the ear to suggest the presence of livestock about the place, but Clem supposes that horses, hens and geese are sleeping in the barn until dawn's light is strong enough to waken them.

Without dismounting he hails the house. 'Harv Golden,' he shouts, and repeats it when the first call garners no response. After some moments there is a flicker of a flame within as an oil lamp is lit. 'Harv Golden,' Clem shouts again, 'come on out here.'

The door opens slowly, not fully, only wide enough for a rifle barrel to protrude and for Harv's voice to carry across the small yard that separates house from gate.

'Who's out there?'

'My name's Clem Rawlings. I ride for the Circle-E.'

There's hesitation before Harv's cautious voice asks him to state his business.

'I've brought Pat Baker back.'

'Pat,' says Harv. 'Is he drunk?' His voice betrays his own doubt at such a possibility.

'He ain't drunk.'

'Has he had an accident?' This question posed by a female voice, Mrs Golden, Clem assumes, which makes him reluctant to shout his next words.

'He's dead,' he tells those inside the house, knowing that no matter how reluctant he is to say it, or unwilling the Goldens will be to hear it, it has to be said.

The door opens wider and, preceded by the barrel of his rifle, Harv Golden steps out into the yard. He makes his way forward, the rifle gripped tightly, a demonstration that he doesn't trust cattlemen visitors. His wife, in a long cotton nightdress with a woollen shawl about her shoulders, follows at a distance. Without taking his eyes from Clem Rawlings, Harv tells her to go indoors. She retreats to the doorway but lingers there, watchful of what might unfold.

When Harv opens the gate Clem gives him the pinto's reins. Harv lifts the sheet covering the pinto's burden and inspects the body. A sigh escapes his mouth, a sound of disbelief mixed with a whole heap of sadness.

'What happened?' he asks.

'He was caught stealing cattle. They hanged him.'

Harv Golden's reaction is exactly what Clem expects. There is anger in the rejection of Clem's words and his raised voice snaps out the words so that they crackle through the greyish light of the oncoming day.

'That boy never stole apples from an orchard.'

Mrs Golden, inquisitive and nervous, calls to her husband. 'What's happened, Harv.'

'It's Pat,' he tells her. 'He's dead. Go inside.' He has no way of knowing if she obeys because his gaze is fixed on Clem, the accusation in his eyes is clear even though the light of day is dim. Ranchers throughout the territory have resisted the incursion of those who have travelled west with the railroad and taken up the parcels of land upon which they intend to build their future, because these newcomers, these nesters, build fences and bar the passage of beeves which have, historically, wandered at will in search of grazing and water. Although, to date, peace has been maintained in the area around Enterprise, there exists between cattlemen and newcomers an atmosphere of distrust and dangerous expectation. Threats have been made against the settlers and this killing of Pat Baker, Harv Golden suspects, is a precursor of more violent tactics aimed at chasing them from the cattlemen's country.

'He was over-branding,' Clem says, telling the farmer the story that would soon be spread around Enterprise.

'Yeah!' There is disbelief in Harv Golden's exclamation. 'You see him do it?'

Clem shakes his head. 'He'd been caught before I got there.'

Harv isn't slow in drawing conclusions from Clem's words. 'But you were there when they strung him up.'

'I was there.'

Harv Golden spits on the ground, his anger, his distaste at the killing of young Pat Baker almost too much to contain. He hefts the rifle in his hands as though using it will purge the boiling blood from his veins.

Clem tugs at the reins of his horse, it steps back as he prepares to turn and ride away. 'Figured you'd want him back here, not left hanging out on the prairie.'

'Where did it happen?'

'Range land south of the Circle-E ranch,' Clem tells Harv. 'Just about sundown,' he adds.

Ruminatively, Harv Golden mutters, almost to

himself. 'He'd be on his way back from the Yates spread.'

Clem doesn't speak although Harv's assessment of Pat Baker's movements is in keeping with his own. He touches his hat in farewell because he can see Mrs Golden is still waiting by the door to her home, half inside, holding the doorpost anxious to learn the details of their farmhand's death.

'Just want you to know,' Clem says, 'Pat Baker wasn't my friend, but he wasn't my enemy either.'

Clem taps his spurs against his horse's flanks and rides away. Behind him he hears Harv Golden's angry voice. 'We aren't forgetting this,' he shouts. 'You can tell Erdlatter that. If killing people is what he wants then that is what he'll get.'

CHAPTER THREE

Breakfast is over when Clem gets back to the Circle-E. Charlie Sow is washing tin plates and tin mugs in a wooden tub outside the cookhouse, knowing that the heat in the now risen sun will dry them while he busies himself with preparations for the next meal. With an air of disgruntlement he watches the young man ride through the gates. Like all ranch cooks he is offended by criticism of his meals and when a hand does not turn up for a meal that is the greatest insult of all. 'If young Rawlings expects a serving at this late hour,' he tells himself, 'he is in for a shock.'

Elsewhere around the compound men are preparing for the day ahead. Carl Pelton and Tiny Duggett are already in the saddle, ready to set out to the north pasture, but they check their mounts and watch as Clem reins in beside Red Hammond. The foreman is passing on instructions to Gus Farley and Slippy Anderson but he is silenced by the appearance of the missing breakfast mouth.

Without dismounting, Clem states his business.

19

'Reckon I'll be moving on,' he tells Red. 'I've got some money due. I'd appreciate you getting it for me while I collect my belongings from the bunkhouse.'

'You'd appreciate,' mimics Red Hammond; his gruff voice holds no hint of humour. 'You'd appreciate!' He runs a thick finger along the scar that runs from the corner of his left eye to the centre of his cheek, then looks around at the rest of the crew who have gathered to listen. 'Well now, I'd appreciate if you got yourself up among those hills and chased a few strays down to the riverside. We've got a herd to round up for trailing to the railhead within two weeks, so this is no time for men to be quitting on us.'

'Even so,' Clem responds, 'quitting is what I'm doing. I've just come back for what I'm due.' He looks over his shoulder. Tiny Dugget is behind him to his right and Carl Pelton to his left. They both wear sour expressions.

'You'll get what you're due at the end of the month along with everyone else.'

'I'm moving on. I want my money now.'

Tiny Duggett nudges his horse so that it moves alongside Clem. He talks to Red Hammond but the words are meant to rile Clem. 'Reckon he just doesn't like the way we dealt with the rustler. Some people just ain't man enough for it.'

Clem doesn't speak and for a few moments there is an uneasy silence. Then Duggett speaks again, still addressing his words to the foreman, still intending to rile young Clem Rawlings. 'Don't know why he's all het up, we done him a favour last night. Everyone knows he has a hankering for the Yates girl. She'll be on the look-out for a new beau now.'

Red Hammond and Carl Pelton grin at the remark but Gus Farley and Slippy Anderson allow no emotion to show. They are older men, accustomed to bunkhouse squabbles and conscious of the fact that it is taboo to get involved in other men's arguments. That doesn't mean they don't have a view on the subject or a bias for one or other of the protagonists, but until the dust settles they will keep their own counsel. Every man has to fight his own battles.

Clem Rawlings seethes at Tiny Duggett, his anger fuelled by the fact that his words are a blunt exposure of the truth. He does like Joanna Yates, indeed his feelings for her are beyond liking and her friendliness towards him had given him hope in the past that she cared for him. But Clem had always had a rival and although Joanna still greets him pleasantly when they meet, Pat Baker had been the one to win her affection. It was their rivalry for Joanna rather than the manner of their employment that effectively created the barrier to any friendship they might have known. Even so, and despite the blow to his own hopes, Clem has nurtured a certain admiration for the pair. Sepp Yates, Joanna's father, is a rancher whose herd is second only in size to that of Nat Erdlatter's. Considering the division that exists between cattlemen and settlers the decision to allow a farm hand to visit his daughter suggests a great deal of argument and compromise all round, and overwhelming determination, he suspects, on the part of Joanna and Pat. It speaks of a strong attachment to each other and, although Clem's hopes have lingered, the passing of time has diminished them.

Now, it seems clear, they are dashed for ever. It will soon be general knowledge that he was among those who lynched Pat Baker and Joanna will never speak to him again. Tiny Duggett, Clem suspects, is having similar thoughts and has thrown the barb specifically to rile him. At first he resists the temptation to respond.

'She's a mighty fine-looking girl,' Tiny continues. 'Might even ride over there myself. Flatter her with the attention of a real man.'

Tiny Duggett does not resemble his name. He is tall, broad and his chest is deep. His head sits on his shoulders like a small boulder and bears a number of small nicks and scars which are the residue of many bar-room brawls. He weighs half as much again as Clem Rawlings but that is the last thing on the young man's mind. He regards Duggett's last words as an insult and launches himself at the bigger man.

The impetus of Clem's attack unseats both men and they tumble to the ground. Tiny tries to throw a punch at his attacker but Clem is clinging tightly to his opponent, preventing his arms from swinging. Tiny curses and uses his strength to push Clem away. The result is a ripped pocket because the young man is still holding tightly to Tiny's shirt. They wrestle for a moment, arms around each other's neck and Clem is forced to his knees. Tiny steps back, giving himself room to kick out at his opponent's head. Clem throws himself backward, sprawls in the dust to avoid Tiny's boot. This gives the big man an opportunity which he doesn't spurn. He steps forward, grips Clem's shirt and pulls his shoulders off the ground. He delivers a vicious punch to Clem's face with his free hand and is about to repeat the punishment when a voice orders a stop.

Nat and Vinny Erdlatter have emerged from the house and are striding across the compound to investigate the cause of the commotion. Nat's voice carries a stamp of authority, the brusque tone expecting prompt obedience. It isn't the fight he objects to; he knows as well as anyone present that bunkhouse dust-ups are an accepted part of ranch life, but he won't tolerate them when the men should be working the beeves.

'Stop that,' he commands.

Tiny Duggett, still holding a handful of shirt, draws back his arm in preparation of delivering another blow to Clem's head.

'I said that's enough,' snaps old man Erdlatter. 'If you want to fight do it on your own time. Right now I'm paying you to gather a herd together. Red?'

The last word is merely an enquiry as to the orders that have been issued to the men but the foreman misinterprets, thinks the boss wants an explanation for the ruckus.

'It's Rawlings,' he begins, 'he's talking of quitting.'

Tiny Duggett sneers. 'Hasn't the stomach for last night's chore.'

His words are spoken over the foreman's continued explanation, his knowing that the reason for Rawlings decision to quit is unlikely to be of interest to the boss. 'I told him nobody quits in the middle of a round-up.'

Clem gains his feet, brushes the dust from his clothing and turns to face Nat Erdlatter whose stone grey eyes are fixed upon him. 'I'm quitting,' he states.

'You work until the end of the month,' declares Erdlatter, 'otherwise you forfeit any money due.'

'You owe me two weeks' pay,' says Clem.

'If you quit before the end of a month you're in breach of contract,' Erdlatter tells him. 'That was understood when I took you on. Now get to work and chivvy the cattle down from the hills.'

Clem's face tingles as a result of the blow he's taken; he thinks there might be blood on his face so he wipes his sleeve across his mouth and cheek before replying.

'You can't do that, Mr Erdlatter. Perhaps you made your own rules when you first came here but now there are laws in Wyoming. You have to heed them just like everyone else. I'm quitting and I want my money.'

Nat Erdlatter's eyes narrow. No one has ever spoken to him in such fashion. He looks at the faces around him. Although the older hands, Gus, Slippy and Charlie Sow, are startled by Clem's words they maintain the same dead-pan expressions of un-involvement that they've displayed throughout the morning's events. Slippy, however, scrapes in the dust with the toe of his boot, a sign of anxiety; he knows too well the ferocity of Nat Erdlatter's temper. Tiny Duggett and Carl Pelton can't disguise their amazement nor hide their pleasure in the anticipation of the boss whipping the young upstart.

Vinny steps forward, his hand drops to the butt of the pistol he carries at his side. 'I'll run him off our land, Pa,' he states. 'I'll plug the sonofabitch if I have to.'

Nat Erdlatter stretches his arm to bar his son's advance. 'Let him have his say,' he mutters. 'He looks like a young man with a full craw. Best let him spit it out.'

'You're right, Mr Erdlatter,' begins Clem, 'there are things that need to be said.' For a moment they stare into each other's eyes and Clem is aware that the cattleman is close to letting Tiny Duggett finish the job that he'd interrupted earlier. 'You're just as wrong to refuse paying the fourteen dollars I'm due as you were last night.'

'Wrong?' snarls Nat, his eyes agleam with the burning light of his temper. 'Wrong to punish a man for stealing from me? Rustlers know the risk they run. If they get caught we hang them.'

'You don't know he was rustling any more than I do. You didn't ask him for an explanation. You didn't allow him to say a word in his own defence.'

'What defence? My men caught him red-handed. Or are you calling my men liars?'

'I'm not accusing anyone of anything. All I'm saying is that Pat Baker was an unlikely rustler and that he should have been handed over to the sheriff. The law should prove the guilt and mete out the punishment.'

'The law? Are you talking about Sheriff Tom Bright? The man I put into office? He does what I tell him.'

'But Pat Baker would have had a chance to speak. You deprived him of that last night and then you deprived him of life.'

'He was a rustler who tried to steal my cattle. His rotting body swinging out there on the range is a greater message to anyone else who thinks they can take my cattle than all the legal words uttered in an Enterprise courtroom.'

'He's no longer swinging from a tree,' Clem tells the Circle-E boss, 'I cut him down.'

'You did what?'

'I took his body back to Harv Golden's place.'

'If you did then you'd better get off my ranch right now.'

'I'm going,' says Clem, 'but remember that Pat Baker wasn't a drifter or a member of a raiding gang; he lived in this valley and was liked by a lot of people. I don't suppose they'll like what you've done.'

'Is that some kind of threat?' asks Nat Erdlatter.

Clem shakes his head. 'It's a fact, Mr Erdlatter. You've said some strong words against the settlers in the past, perhaps they'll judge this as the opening salvo in hostilities against them.'

'I can handle anything that that assortment of riff-raff can assemble against me. If they want a fight I'll accommodate them.'

Clem Rawlings notes the gleam in the old man's eyes, knows that the prospect of conflict appeals to him because he has seen that same gleam whenever the rancher is retelling tales of past skirmishes with rustlers and Indian war-parties.

'I want no part of a range war,' Clem declares, 'especially on the side of the aggressor.' He puts a foot in a stirrup and prepares to haul himself into the saddle.

'What are you doing?' asks Nat Erdlatter.

'I'm leaving,' Clem tells him.

'Have you seen the mark on that animal?' Clem looks at the horse's haunch, sees the burn mark. 'He's got my brand burned into him. You're leaving but you ain't taking my stock with you. Not unless you want to be hanged as a horse-thief.'

There are sniggers from Tiny Duggett and Carl Pelton. Vinny Erdlatter says, 'Get on your way, Rawlings.'

Clem pauses a moment, looks at the faces of those gathered around and finds little encouragement in their expressions. 'The saddle's mine,' he says, determined not to be cowed by the cattle-baron. He unfastens the cinch and pulls the saddle and blanket off the beast's back.

'Now get off my land,' Erdlatter tells him. 'I'll give you an hour, if you're caught on my range any time after that I'll see to it that my men whip you within an inch of your life.'

Clem lifts the saddle on to his shoulder. He remembers Harv Golden's words but doesn't want to tell him what the settler along Westwater had said, doesn't want to make it sound as though the settlers would come seeking revenge for the death of Pat Baker. That would surely lead to a range war which would only produce more needless deaths.

'Times have changed, Mr Erdlatter,' he says. 'I don't think you've heard the last of this.' He hefts the saddle higher on to his shoulder and heads towards the yard gate. No one speaks as they watch his departure until the old man makes a move back to the ranch house. Gus Farley speaks up.

'Reckon now is a good time for me to throw in my hand, too,' he says.

Nat Erdlatter's steel-grey eyes fix on Gus's face, issuing a warning that he will not tolerate further criticism over the lynching of Pat Baker.

'You've been with me a long time.'

'You know cattle pushers, Mr Erdlatter. We never settle in one place too long.'

'Didn't expect it, Gus. Permanent job here for you. You're a good hand.' They are looking hard at each other, neither wanting to say words that worsen the situation but both knowing that the confrontation with Clem Rawlings has opened a rift between them.

'I've been thinking of it for some time,' says Gus. 'Reckon this is a good time. It's as easy for you to hire two new men as one.'

'You're sure about this, Gus?' The implication that Gus's quitting puts him on the opposite side of the fence is not lost on anyone gathered in the yard.

Gus nods. 'You're holding some money for me,' he says. 'I'll take it now.'

Nat Erdlatter stares at him, seems on the verge of a quarrel but eventually says, 'I'll get it from the safe.'

'Keep back enough for two horses,' he tells Erdlatter. 'I'll pick out a couple that haven't been branded while you sort out what I'm due.' As he turns and walks towards the corral he is aware of the anger showing in old man Erdlatter's eyes.

CHAPTER FOUR

In the growing heat of day and burdened by the weight of the saddle, Clem Rawlings is sweating. Although he has put a mile between himself and the Circle-E compound he is aware that he has no hope of being clear of Erdlatter's territory before the expiry of the hour deadline, and when he picks up the sound of following horses he expects it will be Tiny Duggett and Carl Pelton in a hurry to finish off the fight that had been stopped too early. He turns and is surprised when he recognizes the slouched riding style of Gus Farley.

Gus is riding a chestnut gelding and tagging along a smoke-grey horse with a black head. He's not sure how much they are worth, how much he's paid for them, nor how much money is now in his pocket. Nat Erdlatter had betrayed no hint of their value when inspecting Gus's chosen animals, had merely handed over a roll of paper money without comment before walking away. Gus had thrust the money in to his pocket without counting it, thrown his saddle on the chestnut, then ridden away from the Circle-E. At that moment he'd have been hard pushed to give a reason for quitting but instinctively he knew it was the right thing to do.

For nine years he has been earning a dollar a day and found at the Circle-E, his longest-ever period of continuous employment, and until this morning he'd have been content to see out his days pushing cattle for Nat Erdlatter. The old man knows his business, runs a good ranch and is as fair with his men as any cattle boss Gus has ever worked for. That's why he didn't count the money the old man had given him. Nat Erdlatter isn't mean in that way and the money now bunched in Gus's pocket will be every penny he is due. It won't be much: mainly bonus payments earned on cattle-drives to the railhead, but counting it would have insulted Erdlatter and Gus isn't a man to do that without reason.

He drops the grey's reins. 'Saddle up,' he tells Clem, 'and let's get out of here. Tiny's still full of hell and I don't doubt that he's close behind.'

'We're going to have to finish that fight sometime,' says Clem.

'Sure you are but it'll be better for you if it's done on neutral territory. They won't restrict themselves to a fair fight if they catch you on Circle-E land.'

'I'm not afraid of them,' Clem tells Gus.

'No, I don't suppose you are. Anyone who talks to old man Erdlatter on his own property the way you talked to him this morning can't be afraid of much. Or else you're plain dumb.'

Clem grunts. 'Could be the latter,' he tells Gus, then

grabs the rein while slinging his blanket and saddle on the grey. 'Won't the old man come chasing after his horse?'

'It isn't his,' Gus informs him, 'it's yours.'

'How come?'

'Well I can't ride two, can I?' Clem's quizzical expression prompts brusqueness from Gus. 'Quit the jawing,' he tells Clem. 'Just mount up and let's get out of here.' Clem obeys; his questions will keep until they reach Enterprise.

Enterprise is a growing town, many of the newer properties are constructed with brick and are stone-faced as opposed to the old timber buildings with their false-front façades. There are two long streets, Drover Street and Hill Street, which run parallel but are joined by a handful of cross streets so that overall the town is laid out as a series of rectangles. To the basic trade establishments: hardware store, barber, blacksmith and grain merchant, the stalwarts of civilization, have been added a church, a school, a bank and a newspaper. There is a fine hotel, the Enterprise House, and two or three of lesser grandeur where rooms can be rented by the night, the week, or longer if necessary. The Enterprise House stands at the north end of Drover Street, facing back down its entire length as though fixing the town's extent, saying that Enterprise will not pass beyond this point.

Clem and Gus hitch their mounts outside the Prospector Hotel on Hill Street, where they rent rooms for the night. It is reputedly the cheapest rooming house in Enterprise but that doesn't discourage Clem because he intends staying only one night and his purse dictates that he can afford nothing better. Like most cowhands he lives from one pay day to the next, always confident that if one job ends another will be instantly available. Already he owes Gus the price of a horse, although the debt has not been discussed nor is it one that Gus wishes to recoup. The two ex-Circle-E men have come to an agreement that in the morning they will travel north together and seek work on one of the large Montana ranches.

They stable the horses and call in to a small merchandise store to purchase coffee, beans and bacon for the journey ahead and it is as they cross Drover Street that they see Tiny Duggett and Carl Pelton dismount and go into the Prairie Paradise.

'Let's get a beer in the Diamond,' suggests Gus.

Clem sets his jaw with determination. He isn't one to turn away from a fight even if the odds are against him, but he knows there's nothing to be gained by brawling with the hands from the Circle-E.

'I doubt if there's a saloon in town that will welcome us,' he says. 'Erdlatter will have made it clear that we're not to be served in those places where he has influence and we'll be marked as members of the lynching party in the saloons that the settlers use.'

Gus nods. 'Happen you're right,' he agrees. 'Looks like we're stuck with coffee.'

Agatha Grant runs an eating-house on Drover Street. It is a place used by cowboys, nesters and townspeople alike, a place where the portions are generous and the food from fresh-baked bread to beef steaks and the trimmings is a treat for the palate. Both Clem and Gus are regular customers, accustomed to a polite welcome. A card now hangs in one of the small glass frames of the door. The red handwritten letters demand attention: NO SERVICE FOR CIRCLE-E.

Gus reads it with his hand already on the door handle. Beyond, standing near her serving table, he can see Agatha Grant, her expression solemn and determined.

'We're not Circle-E,' says Clem and extends his arm to push open the door.

Gus blocks his effort. 'I think we're tarred with the same brush, Clem. Judging by the look on her face I'd say that Mrs Grant isn't in the mood for listening to our pleas.'

Customers occupy several tables; all faces are turned towards the door, waiting to see how the two cowboys outside will react. It is clear that news of Pat Baker's hanging has spread through the town. The faces demonstrate a mix of expressions; anger, disgust and indignation. No one shows sympathy or friendliness for those at the door.

Clem observes those inside for a moment; his mind jumps to the conclusion that if Agatha Grant's reaction is typical of the citizens of Enterprise then Nat Erdlatter's rash action might bring him more trouble than he expects, and Clem's own parting warning which, at the time, seemed like an empty threat might prove to be significant.

'Come on,' he says, 'perhaps there's nothing to keep

us in this town any longer.'

They cut through to Hill Street, back towards the Prospector Hotel, their minds half-settled on an intention to gather their belongings and ride away from Enterprise. A buckboard passes them; the driver is Seth Hawks, another settler who is farming land along the Westwater. He brings his team to a halt outside Jake Clewson's saloon and hurries inside.

From where they stand Clem and Gus can hear the commotion inside Jake Clewson's saloon. It isn't the noise of a brawl, no sounds of fighting men or breaking glass and furniture, but a cacophony of raised voices as irate men shout out, determined to have their views aired and heard. There can be no doubt as to the cause of their anger even if the exact words don't carry to the two ex-Circle-E men.

Clem takes a step towards the saloon but Gus grabs his arm. 'Nothing to be gained by going in there,' the older man says.

'Don't you feel guilty, Gus? Don't you want to tell them what you saw?'

'Thought you did that when you rode over to Harv Golden's place earlier.'

'I did,' agrees Clem. 'Just feels like there should be more to say.'

Gus rubs the back of his hand across his nose. 'I've been around lynchings before,' he states. 'Sometimes I've been with the mob and sometimes I've been a friend of the victim. Either way, they leave a bad taste behind.'

'And this time?'

A sound escapes Gus, it is neither a laugh of amuse-ment nor a snort of resentment. 'Nothing we say or do will alter what happened last night and now we've got ourselves stuck in the middle. Neither side trusts us so let's move on. We can't change what happened and nothing we can say or do will improve our popularity. They'll always think of us as they do now.'

That final assessment is already lodged in Clem's mind; it is probably the reason he wants to face Pat Baker's friends. When he leaves town he knows that many will think it is from fear of ensuing reprisals, but this isn't true. It is guilt that burdens him, a weight more crushing than carrying his saddle in the midday sun. The guilt, he tells himself, stems from his failure to prevent the hanging, but in addition he remembers that final look that passed between him and Pat, a look that was like a promise which he's unable to fulfil. Although he has no idea what he could have done to save Pat Baker's life he cannot shake the belief that there must have been something. He knows it is impor-tant to him that people should know the truth, and one person in particular, even though he doubts that she will ever again think of him with respect.

Gus is waiting, the sharp eyes in his lined face watch-ing Clem like a hawk, keen to get the younger man out of town, the quicker to banish the deed of the previous night from the deeper reaches of his memory. 'Come on,' he urges, then turns towards their rooming house.

At that moment the doors of Jake Clewson's saloon swing open and half a dozen men step on to the board-walk. They are not arguing but their discussion is serious and each one seems to have a point to make. Harv Golden is among the group and it is he who stops and points at the two cowboys across the street.

'There's young Rawlings,' he says, tugging at the shirtsleeve of the nearest man, attempting, it seems, to propel him forward. 'Now's your chance to question him.'

Indignantly, the man shakes him off but before taking steps towards Clem and Gus he fidgets with his clothing as though Harv Golden's urging has left him in sartorial disarray. In fact, although it is done subconsciously, straightening his waistcoat is a device to draw attention to the badge over the left pocket, a mannerism which announces his credentials to whomever he intends to address in an official capacity.

'Leave this to me,' he tells Harv who, along with the rest of the group, is close on his heels.

'I'm the law in Enterprise,' Tyro Brooks declares as his right hand brushes across the thick moustache drooping either side of his mouth. 'I believe you were present at the hanging of Pat Baker.'

'I was there,' says Clem.

'Need to ask some questions.'

Episodes of Saturday-night hell-raising have ensured that neither Tyro Brooks nor the town jail are strangers to Gus Farley. He growls his contempt of the lawman.

'Rustlers on the range,' he states. 'No business of a town marshal.'

Tyro Brooks moves his head, an acknowledgement perhaps that Gus's interpretation of the duties of respective law officers is correct, but he doesn't spare the older cowboy a glance, keeps his unflinching gaze on Clem.

'If a crime was committed I've got no authority to arrest anyone,' he concedes, 'but it doesn't prevent me investigating and reporting the matter to the sheriff of the county if I think it appropriate.'

'We don't have to tell you anything,' says Gus. 'Come on, Clem.'

Harv Golden appeals to Clem. 'Pat wasn't a rustler. You know it, too, else why would you bring his body out to my place?'

'Guess I was hoping to prevent trouble between cattlemen and yourselves.' Clem knew that all the men gathered with the marshal were newcomers to the territory.

'It's the cattlemen who are making trouble and if we don't hit them hard now they'll think they have a free hand to kill again. We've got to stop them.'

Tyro Brooks turns to face the speaker. 'That's enough of that kind of talk, Jim Welsh. Leave the matter with me and there'll be no more killing or trouble. I'll investigate and inform the sheriff of my findings.'

Jim Welsh spits on the ground. 'Sheriff! Tom Bright is bought and paid for by Nat Erdlatter. He ain't gonna listen to any grievance against ranchers.'

'Don't go talking yourself into trouble with me, Jim,' snaps Tyro Brooks, 'nor attempting to rouse up trouble around town. If I hear that you're provoking ill-feeling against the ranchers you'll find yourself sitting in a cell down at the jailhouse.'

There are murmurs among the men, words to placate Jim Welsh, which allows Marshal Brooks to turn his attention back to Clem Rawlings. 'So will you answer my questions?'

'I told Mr Golden everything I know. I've nothing to add.'

'If I'm going to fill out a report I need the story in your own words,' insists Tyro Brooks.

Clem sighs, resigned to a repetition of the facts. 'We were heading for the ranch,' he began.

'Who is we?' interrupts the marshal.

'Mr Erdlatter, Slippy Anderson, Gus and me. Vinny had raced ahead to show us that his pony was still full of stamina after a full day working on the slopes.' Everyone knew Vinny Erdlatter's character, his ever present braggadocio, so Clem isn't surprised by the derisive expressions which flit across most of the faces around him. 'He was a few minutes ahead of us,' he continues, 'and we caught up with him along a ridge over by the south pastures. He'd met up with Jos Hammond and a couple of the crew. They'd caught Pat running an iron over our brand. They had a rope around his neck when we got there and when Mr Erdlatter had listened to them he said hanging was cattleman's justice. Pat's horse was chased out from under him. That's all there is to tell.'

'Over the south pasture,' Harv Golden says, once more gripping Tyro Brooks's shirt to get his attention. 'That's where you would expect him to be. He was over at Sepp Yates's place last night. Goes there to see the girl, Joanna. Real sweet on her, he was.'

38

Clem shuffles his feet. Tyro asks, 'Are you sure he was there last night?'

Harv Golden nods his head. 'Sepp confirmed it when I spoke to him.'

'Is he in town?' asks Clem.

'Yeah. Him and the girl. Near fainted away, poor thing, when I broke the news.'

It is clear by the way that Tyro pulls at the ends of his moustache that he attaches some significance to the fact that Pat had a bona fide reason for being in that region when he was caught.

'Are you finished with us, Marshal?' Clem asks. He is troubled by thoughts of Joanna and by the knowledge that he is incapable of providing any remedy for her pain.

'One more question,' Tyro Brooks tells him. 'Who whipped the horse from under Pat Baker?'

'We didn't see,' says Gus.

For a moment it seems that Clem will go along with his older companion's remark but at the last moment he changes his mind. He thinks of Joanna's pain and the way he'd been treated by the Erdlatters that morning. He also remembers the gleam in Vinny's eyes when he slapped the pinto's rump with his hat. He has no doubt that Vinny Erdlatter will brag about his part in the lynching of Pat Baker to anyone who will listen to him, so there seems little reason to keep that information to himself.

'It was Vinny,' he says, words which generate further murmurs from the surrounding homesteaders.

'I think I need to involve the sheriff,' declares

Marshal Brooks. 'I'll get a telegram off to him. He'll be here in a couple of days. Meanwhile,' he says to Clem, 'when you get back to the Circle-E you can tell Mr Erdlatter we'll be coming to speak to him.'

'We aren't going back to the Circle-E,' Gus tells him. 'We quit this morning.'

Tyro Brooks examines their faces. 'In that case,' he says, 'I don't want you boys leaving town until you've spoken to the sheriff.'

CHAPTER FIVE

There is nothing elegant about Gus Farley. Whether he is astride a horse, sitting at a card table or, as now, walking down the street, he slouches. His bowed legs reduce his height by several inches and his head seems to be too heavy for his drooped shoulders, so that as he walks his eyes are fixed on the road two steps ahead and when he talks his words appear to be directed at his boots.

'We shoulda kept on riding,' he murmurs. 'Trouble is the only thing we can expect if we stay in Enterprise. We've got no friends here, Clem. Let's just mount up and make our way up to Montana as we planned.'

'Marshal wants us to hang around until the sheriff gets here.'

'Tyro Brooks! He's got no authority to keep us here and he knows it. Besides, Jim Welsh was speaking the truth when he said Tom Bright was Erdlatter's man. The cattlemen elected him sheriff and he'll do whatever they tell him to do.'

Clem can't argue with Gus's assessment but it

doesn't affect his reluctance to leave town. He can't shake off a sense of guilt nor rid himself of the memory of that fleeting exchange of glances with Pat Baker and the belief that it contained a dying man's last thought. Not a plea for mercy but a request, perhaps wanting justice for a wronged man. The more details Clem recalls of that night the less evidence there seems to be of rustling by Pat Baker or anyone else.

'Gus, I appreciate what you did for me this morning but if you want to ride on that's OK with me. I'll be sorry to see you go, but until I've settled things in my own mind I'm not leaving Enterprise. I know I owe you for the horse and I'll repay that debt just as soon as I've got the dollars in my pocket.'

The older cowboy raises his head so that he looks squarely into Clem's face. 'I don't care about the money,' he says. 'That horse is a gift. I'm more concerned about keeping you out of trouble. There's gonna be a war here,' he tells the younger man, 'and there's nothing you can do to stop it. Neither side wants us, Clem, because neither side trusts us and if we get dragged into it neither side will have any pity on us. I'm urging you to leave here because what's about to happen has nothing to do with us. I've been in situations like this before and there are always as many casualties among the innocent as there are among the combatants.'

They stop in the middle of the street. Clem drags a foot in the dust like he's drawing a line of demarcation, as though the decision now forming in his mind is a significant moment in his life. 'I need to go back to where they caught Pat, need to look around, try to figure out what happened there.'

Gus shakes his head. 'If they catch you on Erdlatter's land they'll whip you, Clem.'

'The hanging didn't take place on the Circle-E, it was open range.'

'Leave the investigating to Tyro Brooks,' urges Gus.

Clem ignores him. 'There were no cattle in sight, Gus, only a small fire and, more important there was no sign of the branding-iron that Pat was accused of using.'

Gus rubs at his whiskered jaw aware that he's running out of arguments. The absence of cattle when they were gathered under the hanging tree had not escaped his notice either, but, unlike Clem, he is prepared to believe they had been chased away by Red Hammond and the boys when they apprehended Pat Baker. Whether they did or not, looking for them will only lead Clem into trouble. He likes the boy, wants to steer him away from conflict with the boss of the Circle-E because in such circumstances powerful cattlemen always win.

'What are you hoping to prove?' he asks. 'Pat Baker is dead. Right or wrong, you can't bring him back.'

'I know that, Gus.' There is a flash of anger in Clem's eyes, an anger born of something deeper, more fundamental than Gus's arguments. He knows that the older man's advice is sound and that his urgency for leaving town is to keep them clear of the trouble they will surely encounter when they next meet any Circle-E riders. He also knows that Gus's urging does not spring from cowardice, it is merely that his experience and common logic point to the fact that there is no gain in confrontation. But frustration coils around him like a wrangler's lariat, hampering his thoughts and tightening his guts so that when he speaks again the words rush out in a torrent.

'I think I stood by and let an innocent man hang last night, Gus, and I don't feel good about it. You're right, nothing anyone does can bring Pat Baker back, but if no one does anything then the truth will never be discovered. Perhaps I won't find anything significant, or perhaps I'll prove his guilt, but I've got to take another look around the south pastures. I know you think I'm crazy but I can't turn my back on this thing.'

Gus Farley spits in the dust. 'Can't get a beer in any of the saloons and can't get a coffee in the respectable parlours, I might as well saddle up and ride with you.'

Clem begins to protest but quickly realizes that Gus doesn't want to be talked out of his decision. He clamps an arm around the old man's shoulders and they turn their steps towards the livery stable where earlier they had stabled their horses.

Fred Hardwick's livery stable is sited at the opposite end of Drover Street to the Enterprise House hotel. When Clem and Gus emerge from the narrow connecting alley from Hill Street they find the oldest part of town a hubbub of activity. It is as if a spell of silence has been lifted from the inhabitants of Enterprise and all are now attending to their business with renewed fervour. Bonneted ladies with shawls around their shoulders and baskets over their arms move sedately along the boardwalks, stopping occasionally to exchange gossip with each other or to study the goods on display in the merchants' windows.

The menfolk are more vociferous, their greetings are delivered with loud voices and accompanying guffaws, and their ill-tempered commands to recalcitrant animals overflow with rough voiced oaths. There are many animals in the street: riding-horses tethered to hitching posts outside the various establishments and dray teams pulling creaky wagons, some of which are leaving town heavily laden; others, those that rattle and shake as they proceed slowly along the rutted street, are newly arrived, on their way to the grain merchant or the mercantile store for provisions.

The buggy is almost upon Clem and Gus before they realize they are in its direct line. Gus grips his younger friend's sleeve to draw him to the side of the street but Clem is not easy to move. He is fixed to the spot like an oak with deep roots. Transfixed, he stares at the approaching buggy, recognizes the team of blaze-faced chestnuts and the faces of the occupants beyond. Motionless he remains as the vehicle comes closer and still he doesn't move, not even when the girl stretches her arm across the driver and pulls the whip from its holder. Her face is pale and that paleness highlights the bitterness, the anger in her expression.

Joanna Yates stands and draws back her arm; in a moment she will be within range of her victim. Clem understands her intention, understands her motive and, as her wrist cocks with purpose, can find no cause to fault her. He shrugs Gus aside and waits for the sting of the whiplash.

At the last moment, Sepp Yates grabs his daughter's arm and, despite her struggles and shouts, holds it tightly, preventing her from delivering the blow. When they have passed the ex-Circle-E cowboys he slaps the long leathers against the rumps of his horses and they jump forward with stronger strides. When they are out of range he throws a look behind before attending to Joanna's distress, for she is once more seated, her body slumped forward, her head on her knees.

Sepp Yates's look has been brief but the promise of vengeance it carries is burned into Clem Rawlings's mind. When Gus pulls once more at his sleeve he is still slow to move.

'Looks like you've raised the devil in that girl,' says a voice behind them. It's a gruff voice, one rich with scorn. It is not unfamiliar to Clem because it has issued instructions to him every day for the last two years. Red Hammond is on the gallery outside the Paradise. Vinny Erdlatter is at his side. It is evident that they have witnessed Joanna Yates's arrested act of violence. 'Guess your sweet talk isn't enough for her. Looks like it'll be up to me or Tiny to give her the attention she deserves.'

'You stay away from her,' snarls Clem.

'Come away,' advises Gus, his voice low so that it doesn't carry to those on the boardwalk.

'Hey!' says Red, keeping his tone level, as though he is a voice of reason, 'she'll need a proper man to take care of her. Pat Baker's gone and she made it clear just now that you aren't in the reckoning, so it's the lady's choice, I think.' He spreads his arms wide, an insinuation that he is the obvious candidate.

'I've told you,' says Clem, 'stay away from her.'

'Leave it, Clem,' whispers Gus, 'he's trying to goad you into a fight.'

'I don't take to bums like you telling me what to do,' says Red, his right hand resting on the butt of his pistol, 'and if it wasn't that Tiny wants to pull off your arms and beat you about the head with them we'd be pulling iron right now.'

Never before has Clem Rawlings pulled a gun on a man; he doesn't know how fast he'll be able to draw his Colt or, if he is the quicker, how good his aim will be, but the events of the morning have affected his usual placid demeanour and unexpectedly he reacts to the Circle-E foreman's threat. He steps away from Gus, his hand hovering over the butt of his own pistol.

'Don't hide behind Tiny Duggett,' Clem tells Red. 'If you want a fight then let's get it done now.'

For a moment Red Hammond is silent, not only surprised by Clem's willingness to fight but also startled by the cold determination that shows in his eyes. Then he grins, confident that Clem cannot match his own ability with a gun.

'Never thought you had the guts, kid,' he taunts as he, too, steps into the middle of the street. 'Now,' he adds, 'you're a dead man.'

Eyes fixed on each other they circle, hands close to gun butts, both aware of the hush that has fallen over the townspeople on both sides of the street. Red's arm twitches and Clem responds by slapping his hand against his gun, but before either man can drag his weapon clear of leather another gun is fired; its report shatters the silence.

'Not in this town,' shouts Marshal Tyro Brooks, who has approached unseen. He is behind Red and the Colt he fired in the air still smokes in his hand. 'If you cattlemen want to shoot each other then do it out at your ranch. This community doesn't want killings on the street and I'm here to make sure they get what they want.'

Contempt for the town marshal is etched on Vinny Erdlatter's face but he offers placatory words. 'Just having a bit of fun, Marshal.'

'I suppose you call what happened last night a bit of fun, too?'

'No. That was prairie law, Marshal. Longhorn justice.'

Tyro Brooks grunts; it is a non-committed sound but then he extends his arm and points at Vinny and the Circle-E foreman. 'Need the two of you to come down to my office to give statements.'

'Statements?' echoes Vinny. 'What happened out there was cattlemen's business. Nothing to do with you.'

'You're wrong. I'm making a preliminary investigation for when Sheriff Bright gets here. The farmers along the Westwater have sent for him.'

Vinny and Red exchange glances. Vinny smiles; the prospect of Tom Bright taking any side other than that of the cattlemen amuses him. 'Then let's get it done, Marshal,' he declares, and he and Red Hammond

48

follow Tyro Brooks across the street to the lawman's office.

Annoyed by his own rash behaviour, Clem walks down to the livery stable with Gus.

Clem Rawlings dismounts and squats by the black ash remains of the fire twenty yards from the hanging tree on the south range. Legally, this land doesn't belong to Nat Erdlatter but he has commandeered it, grazed his cattle in the lush meadow to the exclusion of all the other ranchers in this valley and, publicly, no voice has ever been raised against his right to do so. It is good land, watered by several creeks and streams which eventually feed the Sweetwater to the south. To the west, smaller valleys and gulches lead up to the high ground where rich grass fields can be found for summer feeding.

Gus swings his right leg around his saddle horn and watches the activity of his younger partner. He seems relaxed, as though at ease with the situation although he knows that if they are caught here by Nat Erdlatter's crew they will be dealt with without mercy. He shuffles in the saddle, looks to the ridges for the appearance of Circle-E riders, then rubs his stomach as he remembers he has eaten nothing since a hurried, early-morning breakfast. He sees Clem rise to his feet, his face empty of expression.

'Anything?' Gus asks.

Clem's response isn't a direct answer. 'Nobody rustles cattle on their own, Gus, but I didn't hear any suggestion that Pat had company last night.'

'Are there tracks of more than one horse?'

'Sure,' says Clem, 'but they could belong to Red and his crew. There are beef marks, too, but it's difficult to say how old.'

Before leaving town, Gus had tried to convince Clem that returning to this scene would be a futile act, and now he believes the other is beginning to realize the truth of the matter.

'There's always stock grazing this stretch of territory,' he says, emphasizing the hopelessness of trying to learn anything from dirt scuffed up by free-ranging animals.

Clem doesn't answer, moving instead away from the dead ash circle, scouring the ground to right and left as he walks a semicircle some twenty yards from where Gus sits his horse. After a while he stops and gazes westward to where the land begins to fold into rises, ridges and the forested slopes of the Buffalo Hills.

'Do you see something?' asks Gus. He casts another glance over his shoulder to assure himself that they are still alone.

'Someone built a fire,' says Clem when he returns to his horse. 'There had to be a reason for that and the absence of a coffee pot or makings for a meal dismisses the probability that they were preparing to eat.'

It is clear to Gus that Clem needs to empty his mind of the thoughts he has been storing. He doesn't interrupt.

'One man might kill a steer if he is hungry and build a fire to roast the meat, but he wouldn't do it here. This spot is too open and too close to the trail between the

Circle-E and Enterprise.' Clem looks to Gus for confirmation of his assessment.

'If Pat Baker was returning from the Yates's ranch he surely wouldn't be stopping to kill a cow for his supper,' agreed Gus.

'And if he was rustling cattle he wouldn't be fool enough to throw and overbrand a steer at this spot either.' Clem rubs his jaw.

'Something troubling you?' Gus asks.

'Lots of things. Most especially,' Clem adds, 'a branding iron. If the fire was built to heat an iron, where is it? And what happened to the steer or steers that were going to be burned? And what happened to the other rustlers?'

Gus shrugs. He has no answers although he can see the logic in Clem's questions.

'There's a trail over there,' Clem says, pointing towards the distant low hills. 'Looks to have been cut by a hard-pushed twenty head.'

'Fresh?'

'I'm not sure but I mean to follow it. It's the wrong time of year to be driving critters into the hills. It'll soon be time to chase those that have strayed up there back here for the summer round-up.'

'Perhaps they've just been moved to better low-land grazing,' opines Gus, although he has no recollection of any such order being issued, nor any suggestion that Circle-E cattle were grazing in sparse meadows, but he's offered the explanation to distract the younger man from his intention to follow the cattle trail. He rubs his stomach again. 'Might be a long ride,' he says, 'and we'll soon be losing light. What do you say we return to the hotel for a meal and chase those beeves tomorrow?'

Hidden in an isolated stand of cottonwoods 200 yards away Dusty Thoms looks along the length of his rifle barrel and brings the foresight into line with Clem Rawlings's right ear.

'What d'you think?' he asks Rollo Wilson.

'Red just told us to keep an eye on them, not kill them. I think we should get back to town and let him know that they're snooping around. The way the kid's pointing up to those hills, I think he must have seen the trail.'

Dusty lowers the rifle. 'Perhaps we should hang around to see what they do next?'

'I reckon they'll head back to Enterprise. Too late in the day to be following trails into the high country.'

Dusty offers no argument and they spur their horses back towards town.

CHAPTER SIX

Throughout the day the hanging of Pat Baker has been the main topic of conversation in Enterprise. The event has been discussed in every saloon, barber shop, mercantile store and household in the small town. Wherever people gather exclamations of outrage are voiced. Everyone is agreed that the death of Pat Baker, a pleasant, hard-working young man, is a loss to the town. The few precise details which have emerged have united the townspeople in rejecting the accusation of cattle-rustling and, as the initial shock of the lynching dwindles, their anger has become centred on the high-handed attitude of Nat Erdlatter and his son.

Although Agatha Grant remains the only person to proclaim her opposition to the actions of the Circle-E by barring its riders from her eating-house, there has been much talk about reprisals against the cattle baron. Marshal Tyro Brooks has broken up several meetings. One heated discussion threw up a threat of vigilante justice but it had been aired by a voice heavy with whiskey and lacking conviction; however, the lawman knows that in fertile ground a seed once sown has every chance of growing. Temporarily, the home-steaders are placated by his agreement to summon Sheriff Bright to Enterprise and by mid-afternoon most have returned to their farms. Still, an air of uncertainty hangs over the town. It will not take much, he believes, for the town to become a powder keg and for a spark to cause an explosion that will spread a war across the range.

Vinny Erdlatter and those of his crew who are in Enterprise are almost unaware of the animosity that the death of Pat Baker has earned them. Such is their belief in the omnipotence of the Circle-E that even the interview with Tyro Brooks has failed to put a dent in their arrogance. They have no respect for this or any other town marshal and barely hear his speech that no civilized community condones lynching. Afterwards, they split their time between the Prairie Paradise and Diamond saloons, the haunts of other cattlemen who, in accordance with the cowboy's creed, listen to the boasts of the Circle-E riders without expressing favour or criticism of what they have heard. Those who dis-agree with the sentiments expressed by Vinny and Red Hammond simply find another saloon or ride back to their ranch base to spread the news.

The hard-riding Dusty Thoms and Rollo Wilson rein in their mounts outside the Prairie Paradise, where they expect to find Red Hammond. Their entrance is abrupt and noisy. Rollo thrusts apart the swing doors which creak and rattle and draw the attention of every-one in the room. Following a swift, unrewarding scan of the faces at the tables they turn their attention to those few men who are ranged along the bar. Red Hammond is one of that number and he pushes himself away from the counter when he realizes that the two Circle-E riders have something to report. They draw him aside, to the far end of the bar where only a couple of their own men are close enough to hear anything of their conversation. What they have to tell him doesn't please the Circle-E foreman. He berates them for not killing Clem and Gus when they had the opportunity and his immediate reaction is to go in search of the pair and finish them before they become more of a problem.

However, quick as Red Hammond's temper is to rise, it rarely takes control of his mind or blinds him to other possibilities. Without witnesses the deaths of the ex-Circle-E riders can blamed on the homesteaders, which will provide the cattlemen with justification for driving them out of the territory. Perhaps tomorrow, he tells his men, Clem and Gus will be found alone on the prairie and he promises a bonus to anyone who delivers their bodies to him.

Clem and Gus canter into town several minutes in the wake of Dusty Thoms and Rollo Wilson. They restable their horses at Fred Hardwick's livery before making their way to the hotel. The desk clerk, a grey-faced, watchful man, runs his hand over his head as the pair enter the lobby. It seems like a nervous gesture but he manages a quick smile as they approach.

'What time is dinner?' asks Gus.

'The gong sounds at seven-thirty,' the clerk tells him.

'Any time after that is just fine.'

A glance at the wall clock tells Gus that the gong won't be sounding for almost two hours. 'Any time before that would be a whole lot better,' he grunts, then makes for the stairs that lead up to the bedrooms.

'Gives us time to wash up,' says Clem.

'I can wash in one minute flat, especially when there's food waiting for me.'

When they turn the corner and enter the corridor that leads to their rooms, out of the clerk's earshot, Clem speaks again. 'That's the friendliest face we've seen since hitting town.'

'Don't get to thinking that we've become popular,' Gus answers. 'Reckon the hotel's just short of customers and he needs our money. As long as no one threatens to tear down the building because we're staying here he'll do whatever's necessary to get our dollars.'

Gus is partially correct. Herbie Tapscott, the downstairs clerk, is experienced enough in the hotel trade to know that presenting a pleasant face to customers is as important as clean linen in the bedrooms and good food in the dining room, and when you aren't running the best hotel in town – the Enterprise House has that distinction – it is essential to do whatever can be done to attract guests.

On the other hand, thanks mainly to Harv Golden, during the course of the day the attitude of the citizens of Enterprise has become less hostile towards Clem and Gus. They haven't been forgiven for their involvement with the lynching of Pat Baker, but word has spread about Clem's action in cutting down the body and taking it to the Golden farm. His behaviour is in stark contrast to the bitter scorn that has been heaped on to the dead man's memory by everyone else connected with the Circle-E.

'Perhaps other businesses operate on a similar principle,' says Clem.

'What do you mean?'

'Mrs Grant's eating-house opens earlier than seven-thirty. Might be worth seeing if our money is as welcome there as it is here.'

'You saw her face earlier today. Do you think we'll be welcome?'

'What have we got to lose? If she won't serve us we'll come back here. You're the one complaining of hunger.'

Gus doesn't think it a good idea but he shrugs. 'Like you say, what have we got to lose?'

The notice is still fixed in place on the inside of the door: NO SERVICE FOR CIRCLE-E, but the smell of a spicy stew hits the duo while they are yet on the other side of the street. In response, Gus's stomach rumbles.

'I've been a regular customer,' Gus mutters. Clem thinks he might be talking to himself. 'Aggie Grant has no cause to turn me away.' His tongue runs over his bottom lip, already tasting the meal he craves.

Besides beating much of the dust out of their coats and trousers, they are washed, hair-combed and wearing their other shirts. Short of being dandified for a Sunday Meeting social there seems little more they can do to create a good impression. Clem opens the door and removes his hat as he steps inside. Gus, like a shadow, follows.

Agatha Grant's eating-house isn't large. There is room for ten tables although often two or even three are pushed together to accommodate groups greater than four. The popularity of the eating place is guaranteed by the quality of the meals. Although townspeople constitute the greatest portion of her customers, the place also attracts settlers and cowboys.

It is yet early but more than half the tables are occupied. There is a general hubbub of conversation, a little laughter and the regular clatter of cutlery against crockery. At the back of the room Tyro Brooks eats alone. Between him and the door three of the tables are occupied by families and the town doctor shares another with the barber. Two men have seats at one other table, it is the one nearest the door. When Clem studies the men he recognizes Jim Welsh and Seth Hawks. Both men are working land out along the Westwater. They stop their conversation when they see Clem and Gus. Their reaction seems to generate an atmosphere of expectation, and although the room doesn't descend into total silence there is such a reduction of sound as to make everyone forget their food for a moment and turn their attention to the two men who have recently entered the eating-house.

At that moment, coming from the back room where the food is prepared, a girl carries a tray bearing plates, cups and coffee pot. This is Lucy Grant, Aggie's daughter.

'Won't be a moment,' she tells Clem and Gus as she

makes her way to the doctor's table. It is only as she places the plates on the table that she looks back and identifies the new customers. 'Oh!' she says.

'We don't ride for the Circle-E,' Clem tells her but there is little conviction in his voice. If Aggie had meant the notice to be taken literally it would read: NO SERVICE TO THOSE INVOLVED IN THE LYNCH-ING OF PAT BAKER. 'We're not looking for trouble,' he adds.

Clem's voice brings Aggie through from the kitchen. She is a sturdy woman whose greying hair is pinned back in a tight bun. She has a pleasant face although her forehead is permanently creased with frown lines and her grey eyes glint like flint to disguise her natural kindness.

Jim Welsh is the first to speak, still nursing the anger that was in evidence earlier that day. 'That's fine,' he says. 'They don't ride for the Circle-E and they don't want trouble. Just sit them down and feed them, Mrs Grant.'

His sarcasm riles Aggie Grant. 'I'm capable of decid-ing who'll get served in here,' she tells him.

'Sure you are,' he says in a tone that is meant to placate, 'but just because they've chosen to quit the ter-ritory doesn't make them any less guilty of the boy's killing than old man Erdlatter himself.'

He intends to say more, his face is flushed because he has so many grievances he wants to air, but Gus Farley interrupts him.

'You've got your view of last night's happening, Mr Welsh, and I ain't saying you're wrong, but Nat

Erdlatter isn't a bad man. You see him now as rich and powerful and without a care for the well-being of anyone else, but it hasn't always been like that. He's struggled for survival just as you're struggling now and there was no one, neither lawmen nor soldiers around to help him. What he has he's earned and having earned it he won't let it go without a fight. Hanging them is the way rustlers have always been dealt with on this range. Perhaps times are changing, perhaps it'll be for the better, but Nat Erdlatter has been as good a boss as any man I've worked for and I'm not ashamed to say it.'

Silence fills the room, even the children who are eating with their parents have turned their heads in Gus's direction.

'Aggie,' he says, 'I've been eating here since you and Josh and Lucy opened up. I didn't come here tonight to cause embarrassment, I came because I'm hungry but if you want us to go we'll do so without any fuss.'

Again, Jim Welsh speaks, directing his words at Seth Hawks but uttering them loud enough for everyone to hear. 'Who wouldn't want to dine with them? One a veritable knight of the prairie and the other, according to Harv Golden, is almost a hero.'

Gus steps forward, his ire apparent to everyone in the room. 'If you want a fight, Mr Welsh, then step outside now, but lay off the boy here. Clem tried to intervene on Pat Baker's behalf but there was nothing that could be done. Perhaps you think you could have saved him if you'd been there, Mr Welsh, but I don't believe you could have done. In fact, I think you're the kind of man who blusters after the event but is never around when the deeds of men are counted.'

At the back of the room Tyro Brooks rises to his feet. 'Jim Welsh,' he says, 'you talk too much.' He addresses his next words to Aggie Grant. 'It is your decision whether you allow those men to eat here tonight, but if you do I'll be happy to have them join me. I need to talk to them again and this would be as good a time as any.'

Aggie doesn't spend a lot of time pondering the matter. She shrugs her shoulders as though the decision is inevitable and nods for them to take seats alongside the town marshal. Lucy brings them plates of beef stew with vegetables which they devour while talking to Tyro Brooks. They tell him nothing new but Clem suspects that Tyro's invitation is merely a means of defusing the situation between Gus and Jim Welsh. Even so, he keeps to himself his concerns about the absence of a branding-iron, cattle and other rustlers. Nor does he tell the marshal of his intention to follow the unlikely trail that he and Gus have found. If Tyro Brooks means to investigate the scene of the lynching he will find it for himself.

'Sheriff Bright should be in town in a couple of days,' Tyro tells them. 'His questions, I suppose, will dig deeper than mine.' His hard stare makes it clear that that he knows they aren't telling him everything. 'Interesting to note,' he adds, 'that you tried to intervene on Pat Baker's behalf.'

He is referring to Gus's defence of Clem when arguing with Jim Welsh.

'It weren't nothing,' Gus says. 'Just that Pat has worked around here for some time, didn't seem any need for him to be rustling cattle.' Knowing that Gus retains a sense of loyalty to his former employer, Clem doesn't want to say that Nat Erdlatter didn't give Pat the chance to deny the charge.

Tyro is still watching the faces of the other two closely but when Lucy arrives at their table he relaxes. 'If that's all you have to tell me I guess I'll leave it to the sheriff to sort out what happens next.'

'I enjoyed the food,' Clem tells Lucy as she gathers up the empty plates. She smiles in acknowledgement of the compliment but it is hesitant, as though she isn't sure that he is the sort of man with whom she should be sociable. When she returns with a coffee pot she seems more comfortable with the presence of Clem and Gus: her cheeks show a little colour and her smile carries a little more warmth.

'Quite a girl,' says Tyro Brooks when she's gone back to the kitchen. 'Helps out at the schoolhouse during the day and helps her mother in this place at night.'

This isn't news to Clem and Gus, isn't news to anyone who has lived around Enterprise for any length of time. The Grants are a respectable and hard-working family whose circumstances were at low ebb when they arrived in Enterprise in 1867. Josh Grant is a cripple, the lower part of his body paralysed by a bullet that nicked his spine during the second battle at Bull Run. Before the war he worked in a timber mill but such manual labour is now impossible. They moved West to aid his recuperation and it fell upon his wife, Aggie, to eke out what little money they had brought with them.

She hit upon the idea of baking bread to sell to her neighbours and when that proved popular added pies and cakes. Within two years she had moved the family into the larger premises which now was the eating house. Josh worked in the kitchen, preparing the food, washing the dishes and every other task that he could undertake until a chance conversation with the editor of the *Enterprise Bugle* brought him fresh employment as the print setter. It didn't replace his work at the eating house, instead it extended his working day.

Lucy had been barely thirteen when she arrived in Enterprise, now she is a composed young woman who combines her mother's toughness with a natural compassion for the misfortunes of others and a smile that men would fight for the right to have bestowed on them. She has no formal training for her role at the schoolhouse but, with the guidance of Mrs Taylor, the appointed schoolma'am, she tutors the children in her charge with the fundamental facts of arithmetic, English and American history.

People have come and gone while the three men have talked and eaten and the lamps are lit when it comes time to pay the bill.

'It's a bad business,' Aggie Grant says to Gus Farley, 'and everyone talks as though the violence is not yet over. Some say that this is just the beginning.'

Gus nods. He thinks of Jim Welsh and knows that it just needs one like him on each side to set the guns blazing. Foolish, dangerous men. He says goodnight and follows Clem and Tyro outside.

The few people still about at this hour are a hundred yards down Drover Street. Gus rubs his hand over his mouth as he gazes down towards the cattlemen's saloons where a few lanterns are lit and the low drone of voices mingled with the tinny playing of a barroom piano remind him that his needs are only partially satisfied.

'A meal like that deserves a glass of beer,' declares Gus.

Tyro leaves them, claiming he has things to do in the office.

Clem says, 'Perhaps we'll get a bottle in the hotel?'

Gus grumbles at that idea. 'Need to lean on a counter, Clem. Beer doesn't taste like beer unless you're in a saloon.'

Clem grins. Gus has uttered the same creed many times in the past. 'It's probably safer to go to Jake Clewson's saloon.' He's thinking aloud and even as the words come out of his mouth he's thinking that if Jim Welsh is in there the welcome they get might be no different from that which awaits them in the Diamond or Prairie Paradise. But Gus sets off down the middle of the street with his accustomed shuffling gait towards the nearest alleyway that will take them through to Hill Street.

Clem is five paces behind his older companion when a gunshot shatters the stillness of the balmy night. He hears Gus curse and sees him fall to the ground. As Clem does likewise a second shot cracks in the night and he feels the wind of the bullet as it passes over his head. The shooter is behind them, firing from a gap between buildings that lead on to the open range.

'Gus?' Clem calls, anxious that his friend has been hit.

'I'm OK.' The words are followed by a squirming movement as Gus snakes forward towards the protection of a water trough. Two more shots kick up dirt close to his body. He curses, draws his pistol and sends two slugs of his own in the general direction of his attacker.

With the gunman's fire mainly concentrated on Gus, Clem has had the opportunity to pinpoint his location. The telltale gun flashes provide a useful target and Clem fans the hammer of his Colt four times; the speeding bullets rip into the wooden frame of the building that is sheltering their assailant.

For a few moments Clem and Gus know nothing but the darkness of the night, the echo of gunshots and the smell of gunpowder. They lie silently in the middle of the street, watchful for movement and a renewed attack. It doesn't come but behind them, from the opposite boardwalk, the sound of running footsteps commands their attention.

'Put up your guns,' shouts Tyro Brooks. 'This is the law.'

Other townspeople have ventured closer now that the shooting has stopped and they cluster around to listen to Clem's and Gus's account of the attack. In the gap where the shooter waited in ambush they find a handful of spent casings but no other clue as to his identity or where he has now taken refuge.

Marshal Brooks promises to investigate the incident but neither Clem nor Gus expect him to uncover their would-be slayer; both cattlemen and homesteaders have grievances against them.

'Still want that drink?' Clem asks.

'More than ever,' Gus replies, and they go on their way to Jake Clewson's bar.

There is no light at all in the narrow gap between the buildings. Gus's eyes are fixed on the ground two steps ahead but it is too dark even to see the ground. Clem's mind can't settle. One second he pictures Pat Baker swinging on the end of a rope and Nat Erdlatter riding away, uncaring of the kicking man whose death he has ordered. Then he sees the anger in Jim Welsh's eyes, there is fear there too, in a man who will be happy to incite others to violence as long as he is far away when it happens. Next it's Joanna Yates with a whip raised and his inability to move away from the lash. If her father hadn't grabbed her arm she would have delivered the blow, would have scarred him for life, but he'd just stood and waited for the sting. Up ahead, to the right, something moves.

'Gus,' Clem's whisper is sharp and hoarse.

'What?' asks Gus as though the word has pierced his own deep thoughts.

'Someone is in the shadows. Over to the right.'

'How many?' Gus whispers; his hand has slipped to the butt of his pistol.

'I don't know.'

They've stopped now, uncertain whether to go forward or back. Perhaps, if there is only one man, he is merely a drunk who has stumbled into the alley to throw out the contents of his stomach. But Clem dismisses that possibility. No one is stumbling about, whoever slunk into the shadows did so as silently as a snake and is now waiting for Gus and him to get closer.

Gus has drawn his gun. Clem does likewise. A voice, barely audible, reaches them.

'Gus.'

'Who is it?'

'Shhh.' The figure moves, beckons the two onwards.

'Who is it?' Gus asks again.

The man steps forward, a gangling shape in a wide-brimmed hat.

'Slippy,' Gus says. 'Is that you, Slippy?'

'Shhh,' the figure admonishes again and when he takes another step closer both Gus and Clem know for sure that it is Slippy Anderson. 'It's dangerous for me to be seen talking to you,' he tells them, 'but I wanted to tell you to get out of town. When you quit the Circle-E Red became determined to whip you good like the old man threatened if you are caught trespassing, but now it's worse. Since learning you've been back to the south meadow he's put a bounty on your heads.'

Clem wants to argue the point that being on the south meadow isn't trespassing but he can see that Slippy is nervous and wants to be away. He pats his old comrade's shoulder to show his appreciation for the risk he's taken.

'Take care, boys,' whispers Slippy. 'Don't let him catch you. He has people watching you all the time. He knows you've eaten in Aggie Grant's house tonight and he's angry about that, too. Can't understand why she let you in but barred him. He's angry and full of whiskey. There's no knowing what he'll do next.'

CHAPTER SEVEN

Clem and Gus deduce from Slippy's message that Red Hammond has had them under observation all day, but they can't decide whether he is obeying Nat Erdlatter's orders or acting on his own initiative. What they do agree, however, is that the Circle-E is too busy and too short of crew for men to be assigned to follow them around indefinitely. Perhaps now they've all gone back to the ranch, giving Slippy the opportunity to pass on a warning.

There are no swing doors at the entrance of Jake Clewson's saloon, just two tall doors the top half of which frame frosted glass. As usual at this time of day, the doors are closed keeping the noise and smoke within, although both tumble out on to the street whenever a client enters or leaves the building. Gus causes it to happen when he grabs the round knob and thrusts the door open. Clem follows him across the threshold.

They are greeted by jangling notes from an ill-played piano. From the far end of the room the forced, coarse laugh of a working girl rises above the general din of conversation. The sound of bottle against glass mixes with the slap of cards on a table and the scuffing of boots across the wooden floor. It takes a moment for their eyes to become accustomed to the smoky gloom of the place and they are halfway to the long counter before they realize that their entrance has been noted by many of the occupants and that their progress is subject to silent scrutiny.

Most of the people in the room are townspeople, many of whom have an opinion about the lynching of Pat Baker, but fewer than a handful have any personal interest. Nonetheless, the rare appearance of cowboys in Jake Clewson's saloon is a noteworthy occasion and these particular men add spice to the event. The barman, a big, broad-shouldered Irishman who has come this far west by laying tracks for the Union Pacific railroad, wears a white shirt with armbands around his biceps and pearl-inlaid cuff links at his wrists. A buttoned waistcoat with a gaudy design in reds and blues covers most of his chest and a black ribbon is tied around his neck. The remains of his dark receding hair is slicked back with some salesman's top dollar lotion. He looks to his left as the pair approach. Jake Clewson, cigar in mouth and hands in his trouser pockets gives a slight nod with his head.

'What'll it be, gents?' asks Mahoney, the barman.

'Two beers,' says Gus, he leans over the bar while the order is filled.

Jake Clewson removes his hands from his pocket and rests the cigar on a tin plate that stays on the counter for just that purpose. Clutching the long lapels of his jacket, he leaves his post and saunters towards the other end of the bar, casually nodding and smiling as though on a general sweep of the room to greet each of his regular customers. He reaches Clem and Gus at the exact moment that Mahoney places their beers before them.

'I don't often get the chance to welcome any of you cattle-pushers to my premises these days,' says Jake. He is standing between Clem and Gus, has placed a hand on the back of each, the gesture as friendly as the words.

Clem puts his glass on the bar, has anticipated Jake Clewson's intention from the moment he took the cigar from his mouth. 'If you want us to leave just spit it out,' he says.

Clewson grins. 'Don't be so touchy, young man. I don't see any reason for you to leave. I'll admit there's been some tough talk against cattlemen in here throughout the day but considering the event of last night that's not surprising. A lot of people here liked Pat Baker.' He turns to gaze around the room. 'Those men there, for instance,' he indicates a table where four men are playing poker: young men, two of whom Clem recognizes as a clerk at the mercantile store and a carpenter studying his trade under his father, 'were especial friends but they aren't the kind to seek vigilante revenge. No, Clem – it's OK if I call you Clem, isn't it?' Without pausing for a reply he says, 'No, all the firebrands have gone back to their farms for the night.' He pauses at that point, shakes his head as though mystified by a thought. 'Funny thing, but when hatred is being drummed up it is seldom by the family or friends. If they intend to take the law into their own hands they tend to just get on with it. It seems to me that howling for mob justice is done by those taking advantage of a situation to gain their own vengeance.' He laughs, scorning himself as a philosopher.

'What's your point?' asks Gus.

'My point is that not every hand has been turned against you in this town and that as this is a place of business you are welcome to spend your money here.'

'But?'

'But if your presence leads to unpleasantness my sympathies will be with my regular customers.'

'Fair enough,' says Clem and takes the first drink from his glass.

'That's right, boys,' says Jake. 'Drink up.' He returns to his favoured spot at the far end of the bar.

They have a second beer before returning to the hotel. Clem wants an early start in the morning, wants to devote as much time as is necessary to trail the bunch of cattle that was driven across the south meadow. Gus doesn't argue. He's had a good meal and some beer, which is a lot more than seemed likely a few hours earlier.

Combined with the multitude of thoughts that fill his mind, the warmth of the night keeps Clem from sleep. He leaves his bed and stands by the open window. Under the dark-purple sky Hill Street is a long black smudge. All the lamps have been extinguished.

Nothing moves. He relives the events and conversations since Vinnie Erdlatter signalled to them from the ridge. It seems that no life existed for him before that moment. His mind fixes on minor things, such as Pat Baker's pinto looking back to see why his rider was no longer in the saddle; Harv Golden's wife half-hidden in their doorway, fearful of his visit; the look on Seth Yates's face and his daughter doubled over, head on her knees as their buggy left Enterprise.

Twenty minutes later he is back at the window wondering if the sky is lighter, sure that the street is darker, and more conversations run through his mind: Tyro Brooks wanting more information for the sheriff, Jim Welsh wanting confrontation with the cattlemen.

Another forty minutes and he's sure the sky is lighter. For a moment something moves below. A creature of the night, he assumes, grabbing the opportunity to scavenge in town while everyone sleeps. Whatever creature it is he doesn't see it again and his thoughts settle on his scuffle with Tiny Duggett at the Circle-E, Nat Erdlatter's threat to have him whipped within an inch of his life if caught trespassing, and Slippy Anderson's warning that Red Hammond means to make good that threat.

He looks again at the sky, convinces himself that there is a pinkiness attributable to the rising sun. He breathes in the morning and a frown creases his forehead. He sniffs and recognizes the unmistakable tang of smoke. His eyes scour the empty street below but he finds nothing. Then a wisp, indistinct at first, rises above the opposite buildings. The longer he watches the more sure he becomes that somewhere on Drover Street a building is on fire.

'Gus,' Clem shouts as he bangs with his fist on his friend's door, 'there's a fire on Drover Street. Raise the alarm.'

The sounds of a disturbed sleeper emanate from the room beyond and Clem hopes that he has done sufficient to rouse the other to full wakefulness, but he dare not linger: fire will spread quickly and will devastate the mainly timber-built buildings along Drover Street. In a matter of seconds he is outside and racing for the nearest access to Drover Street. 'Fire,' he yells as he runs, but he has no way of knowing if anyone is responding.

The spiralling smoke is clear to see now and when he emerges on to Drover Street the glow from rising flames can be discerned. It registers with him that the building ablaze is the Grants' eating-house. He yells the dreaded word, 'Fire', and prays that it will bring assistance quickly. He is grateful that the night air is still, it might prevent the fire from spreading to the buildings at either side of the eating-house.

Suddenly a figure, wraithlike, emerges from the darkness of the night and stumbles towards him. Agatha Grant, in a white night-shift, her greying hair flying loosely in her wake, grips Clem's arm with her right hand and points at her home with her left.

'Lucy,' she says. 'Her father can't help himself.'

She starts to run back towards the house but Clem prevents her. 'The fire alarm,' he tells her. 'It must be sounded. We need everyone out to fight the fire.'

'Yes,' she says, but doesn't realize that he wants her

to summon the townspeople.

'Go,' he says and pushes her down towards the centre of the street where he supposes the emergency bell will be situated.

'Yes,' she says again but can't turn her head from the sight of the flames which are now shooting high into the air at the rear of the building.

'Go,' insists Clem. 'I'll get Lucy out.'

Then he is gone, not knowing if the shock will keep Agatha rooted to the spot or how soon other men might gather to form a bucket chain to douse the flames.

The front door is open, Agatha's means of egress, but also the cause, he believes, of the fire's strength, the source of the draught that fans the flames. There is smoke within, not immediately as he enters but further into the room, forming a grey blanket, obscuring his view of the far wall and the position of the door that leads through to the kitchen and family rooms beyond. There are upstairs rooms but logic tells Clem that Josh Grant will never have seen those.

'Lucy? Josh?' he calls, but receives no answer. Already he can taste the smoke in his mouth, can feel its tickle in his throat. He throws his left arm over his brow as some sort of protection for his eyes and heads to where his memory believes the door to be. His estimation is wrong by several feet but a series of bumps and crashes from the room beyond help him find the doorway.

Through the smoke an orange glow from high-leaping flames gives an eerie appearance to the room beyond. Now there is heat as well as smoke and Clem can hear someone coughing, desperately trying to clear the cloying smoke from their throat.

'Lucy?' he says again but the smoke stifles the sound of his voice, and taking deep breaths is now becoming painful.

A low, rasping cough sounds ahead and at that moment a great flame leaps towards the ceiling, giving Clem a glimpse of Josh Grant. He is on the floor, lying on his side, his wicker wheelchair is also on its side and flames lick at it. Clem steps forward to go to the invalid's assistance but his foot connects with an obstacle on the floor and he falls, his head striking Josh Grant's legs.

The heat is intense and the flames have burned through parts of the wall. Clem suspects that this part of the building might soon collapse and knows he has to work fast if he is to get the man to safety.

'I'll get you on to my shoulder,' he tells Josh.

Josh's red-rimmed eyes are barely opened, he is coughing, spluttering, but his arms wave Clem away. He is pointing behind Clem and gesturing at something on the floor.

The thing on the floor, the obstacle that tripped Clem, is Lucy Grant. She is unconscious. There is blood from a head injury she's sustained by falling against a table when her father's chair capsized. Clem's dilemma is obvious, in the circumstances he can only help one person out of the fire.

'Save Lucy,' her father tells Clem.

'I'll come back,' Clem tells him and ignores the

other's head-shake.

Lucy Grant is a slender girl but transporting her dead-weight from a smoke-filled room is not an easy task. The urgency of the situation strips from Clem any need for gallantry. He puts her over his left shoulder, her arms dangling down his back, thus leaving his right arm free to feel his way back to the outside door. To Clem, the battle through the throat-burning, eye-smarting denseness seems to take an eternity, but in fact he carries the girl for less than two minutes. When he stumbles through the door and out on to the street there is a shout of wonder from those standing near. It isn't until he lays Lucy on the road that he realizes that the townsmen have answered the alarm and are beginning to fight the fire.

Doc Polworth is on his knees beside the girl almost before she's off Clem's shoulder.

'I'll see to Lucy first,' he mutters, 'then I'll take care of you.'

'I've got to go back,' Clem tells him.

'Back! You can't go back in there.'

'Her father's still there. I told him I'd go back.'

'Don't be foolish, man.'

But Clem is on his feet and he plunges his hands into a nearby bucket and douses his face with the water he scoops out. He sees Agatha Grant hurrying forward to the place where the doctor is tending her daughter. Someone has thrown a shawl around her shoulders but she is probably unaware of the fact.

Gus is part of a bucket chain that is throwing water on a neighbouring building. He calls to Clem but his young friend fails to hear. He is too busy soaking a blanket which he throws over his head before rushing back inside the burning building. Gus watches in disbelief.

Inside the burning building the build-up of smoke is visually impenetrable. Clem goes forward by instinct, looking for the glow of the fire to guide him back to Josh Grant. The heat is so intense that the blanket he soaked before re-entering is already dry. Still he keeps it around his head for protection, but against what he doesn't know. He can see the flames now and he can hear the crackling of the burning timbers and even the occasional hiss as a bucketful of water is thrown against the outside wall.

Most of the back room is now aflame because, as he suspected, part of the wall has collapsed and fallen inward. Clem's hope has been to use the wheelchair in his rescue bid but that is not to be. The wheelchair is in flames and, more critically, so is Josh Grant.

Josh hasn't moved while Clem has taken his daughter out of the burning building. He lies on his side with his eyes closed. His mouth is partly open and his tongue protrudes, submitting, it seems to Clem, to the oncoming agony of death. A burning spar has fallen across him and the first flames are leaping from the sleeve of his nightshirt. Instantly, Clem thrusts aside the burning timber and smothers those flames with the blanket.

'I'm here,' he tells Josh. There is no reply but Clem isn't yet prepared to believe that he is too late. He knows he won't be able to lift Josh on to his shoulder

as he did with Lucy, the dense smoke is making it difficult for him to breathe and he knows he cannot
summon up the necessary strength to lift Josh from the
floor. He puts his hands under the other's arms and
begins to drag him backwards away from the flames.

The heat is almost unbearable. It seems to Clem that
all the moisture has been drawn from his face, that his
skin is about to blister or become crisp and crumble
into dust. His lungs feel full and tight, he needs a deep
breath of clean air but when he opens his mouth it is
filled with smoke and he begins to cough. He releases
his hold on Josh Grant and sinks to his knees. A few
seconds of rest, he tells himself, then he must make
another effort. But he coughs again when he makes
the effort, every exertion weakens him further. The
lack of clean air is proving too much for him. He is
aware of nothing but the orange-tinged blackness of
smoke and the weight of the man he holds.

Once more he summons the resolve to get Lucy's
father out of their burning home, once more he grips
him under the arms and pulls and as he does so he
hears someone cough behind him.

'Clem!' The voice is muffled but is unmistakably that
of Gus Farley.

Clem stamps his foot to signal his position and a few
seconds later the older man rests his hand on his shoulder. Together, coughing, wheezing and moaning they
pull Josh Grant from the building. Like his daughter
before him he is placed in the road for the doctor's
attention.

Clem and Gus lie side by side, their eyes red and

their faces black. 'You're a crazy man,' Gus tells his comrade.

'You went in there too.'

'Then I must be crazy.'

Someone hands each of them a tin mug of water. It is Jake Clewson, who says, 'Such crazy men are always welcome in my saloon.'

CHAPTER EIGHT

'You the fella that saved Josh Grant?' Fred Hardwick is watching Clem as he throws his saddle on the grey in the yard behind the livery stable. Gus is over by the corral rail attending to his chestnut.

'We were there.' Clem's answer is non-committal; he doesn't know the stableman's motive for asking the question; whether or not he bears a grudge against him over the lynching of Pat Baker.

'Likely he'd have perished if you hadn't done what you done.' Fred is gazing at the young cowboy, taking note of the smudges that no amount of rubbing has been able to remove from his cheek and brow. Only time will remove them, just as only time will clear away the clogging sensation in his chest. He coughs, as he has done ceaselessly since coming out of the inferno, and if smoke poured out of his mouth he wouldn't have been surprised. As it is, he doubles over as a slash of pain sears inside his chest.

'Seems to me the whole town is in debt to you,' says Fred as he steps forward and runs an experienced

81

hand down the grey's foreleg. The two men straighten up simultaneously, their eyes meet over the grey's back. 'If the fire had spread then some people might have died,' Fred continues. 'You couldn't be everywhere, could you?'

Clem can detect neither cynicism nor humour in the stableman's words. He fastens the cinch and gathers the bridle from the post on which he'd hung it.

'Tom Bright won't get here before tomorrow,' Fred tells him as though there is an obvious progression from last night's events to the arrival of the sheriff. 'That'll give you two days' start. If anyone comes seeking you I'll tell them I'm not expecting you to return 'til late tonight.'

Clem finishes with the harness and turns his attention to Fred Hardwick.

'Gus and I aren't quitting Enterprise,' he says. 'Do you think we're running out without paying our bill?'

'Bah!' Fred is exasperated. 'Do you think I'm going to starve for the ten bits you owe me? I'm telling you to git for your own good.'

'If there's going to be trouble with the settlers I reckon we have to face it.'

'Listen to me,' says Fred, and though his voice is low it carries an edge of urgency. 'You've got more to worry about from the Circle-E. Everyone knows that Tom Bright is the cattlemen's sheriff, but next year is election year and if he wants to keep his office he's going to have to do something to appease the newcomers. There are a lot of them in the territory now, and gaining their vote is going to be as important to him as the ranchers'.'

Leading the chestnut, Gus Farley joins them, curious about their conversation.

Clem needs the liveryman to give a clearer explanation.

'They'll come to a compromise,' Fred Hardwick says. 'To placate the settlers someone will have to be punished for Pat Baker's death. It isn't going to be Nat Erdlatter but he's got two men he can blame and whom all his riders will attest were the instigators.' He looks meaningfully from Clem to Gus and back again. 'I'm not guessing,' he tells them. 'It was voiced by Circle-E riders in the Diamond, last night.'

'But if we flee we look more guilty,' says Clem.

'If you get across the border there is nothing they can do to you. The townspeople won't believe the Circle-E story but no one can testify on your behalf because nobody else was there. Take my advice, lad,' there is an urgent tone to Fred's voice, 'get going now and don't come back.'

Gus and Clem mount up and ride away from the livery stable in silence. The smell of smoke and burned wood permeates the town and it is stronger when they come from the back of the stables into Drover Street. As they approach the building that had been Grant's eating-house they can now see that the front wall is the only one that is still complete, although it is black with soot and smoke. Seeing the devastation in daylight brings home to Clem the recklessness of his earlier actions. Going in a second time had been madness, and when he looks across at Gus the older man slowly shakes his head, a silent concurrence with the thought.

A buggy stands beside the burnt shell of the building; the passenger is talking to one of the townswomen, learning the full story of the fire. The passenger is Joanna Yates. So involved is she in the details that are being disclosed that she doesn't see Clem and Gus as they pass at walking pace. Beside her, in the driving seat, her father watches them with a closed expression. When they are beyond the buggy they touch spurs to their horses' flanks and ride out of town.

Fred Hardwick's revelation that he and Gus are to be framed for the lynching is on Clem's mind. He discusses it with Gus as they ride.

'Old man Erdlatter won't be pleased if Sheriff Bright doesn't support the view that he has the right to hang cattle-rustlers,' Gus tells him, 'and I'm not sure that Sheriff Bright has the courage to buck the man who made him sheriff in the first place.'

'But is it true that the settlers might be strong enough to vote their own man into office?'

Gus thinks for a moment. 'Possible,' he says, 'and if Erdlatter has already hatched a compromise then it seems likely. It's for certain that he won't want to go to prison or lose any of his hands because the settlers are agitating for justice.'

'You should go back to the Circle-E, Gus. Mr Erdlatter would rehire you. He's angry with me, not you.'

Gus shakes his head. 'I've never gone back to any place in my life. Ain't gonna start now.'

'Then ride on to Montana. Take Fred Hardwick's

advice: get across the border.'

'Is that what you're gonna do?'

'I can't, Gus. Don't ask why 'cos I don't know. I know it makes sense to ride clear of this territory but I can't shake away the thought that there is something I need to do for Pat Baker. Perhaps following that cattle trail will give me some answers.'

Once again Gus shakes his head, conveying again the message that his young comrade is crazy. 'We agreed to go to Montana together, didn't we?' Clem nods. 'Then when you're ready to go that's when I'll go.'

By this time they can see the tree upon which Pat Baker was hanged. The place is peaceful now, making it hard for Clem to remember the few frenzied minutes that ended in the young man's death, but the charred patch of ground where the fire had been is still visible and the sight of that smudgy blackness has an effect on his chest and throat. He coughs, doubling over, trying to relieve the ache in his chest. He hides his pain from Gus by riding on, seeking again the trail he'd found of the running steers.

The horse-prints that show alongside the cattle tracks are a clear indication that the beeves didn't wander in that direction of their own accord. Wherever their final destination is, someone intended they should go there. Clem points ahead to the western hills.

'They're up there somewhere, Gus. Let's go and find them.'

They follow the trail without difficulty because

twenty running cattle do a good job of scuffing the top off dry ground. The trackers know it will be more difficult if the trail leads into rock-hard canyons, but it's an even chance that it will stay on the grassland and swing south towards the grazing land around Blackwater Creek. The drawback with that idea is that Sepp Yates turns his cattle out there. Like the south meadow, it is free range but just as Nat Erdlatter is the accepted user of one, so Sepp Yates is the user of the other. It's not unknown during dry summers for the Circle-E to push cattle along Blackwater Creek, but not without informing Sepp Yates of their plan. This year, however, Gus is certain that the Circle-E has had grass and water a-plenty for their cattle.

Before long they cut across the buggy-rutted road that leads to the Yates place. Beyond this the ground becomes less flat, rising in smooth swells that lead on to higher, heavily wooded hills. They rein in their horses and Clem stands in the stirrups to ease his legs and to give him the chance to scout the land ahead. The cattle trail, which is still clearly visible, wends west towards the higher ground.

'They haven't gone to the Blackwater,' Gus says.

Clem agrees as he steps down to poke around a pile of cattle dung. 'Two days,' he tells Gus. 'Three at the most.'

Gus grunts an acknowledgement but his attention is focused on a stand of trees high on his right.

'What is it?' asks Clem.

'Thought I caught a flash,' but he doesn't finish his sentence.

Simultaneously a rifle shot sounds from among the very trees that have attracted Gus's attention and the cowboy yells and drops out of his saddle.

'Gus,' calls Clem but he is given no chance to reach his stricken companion. From the trees come three horsemen, their identities are well known to Clem. Too late, Slippy Anderson's warning now fills his mind. It has only been a handful of hours since they spoke in the dark alley between Drover Street and Hill Street but first the fire and now tracking cattle have made him forget the caution.

Tiny Duggett, Carl Pelton and Rollo Wilson are armed. Clem has no doubt that they will shoot him down if he goes for his gun. In a moment they have him surrounded, upon each face an expression of evil triumph. Carl Pelton carries a rifle so it is he, Clem supposes, who has shot Gus. Gus is on the ground, still and heavy like a toppled sack of potatoes.

'Mr Erdlatter told you to stay off Circle-E land,' says Tiny Duggett. His grin tells Clem that he knows this is open range but he won't let that stand in the way of dishing out the punishment he believes Clem deserves.

Clem says it anyway. 'We're not on Circle-E land and you've got no reason to shoot Gus. Mr Erdlatter won't be pleased when he hears what you've done.'

Tiny brings his right leg over his horse's head and slides to the ground. He puts his pistol into his holster. 'What is there for Mr Erdlatter to know? No one here knows what happened to Gus. As far as Mr Erdlatter knows you and Gus have left the territory.'

'You think I won't tell him?'

'You!' Tiny laughs. 'Mr Erdlatter told me to whip you within an inch of your life but I forgot to bring a ruler with me.' This brings chortles from Carl Pelton and Rollo Wilson. 'But,' he goes on, 'I did bring this.' Coiled around his saddle horn is a thick black bull-whip. He grips the short handle and with a flick of his wrist uncurls the tapering lash displaying its full length, allowing Clem to imagine the pain he will be subjected to when the cord slices his body.

Rollo Wilson and Carl Pelton back their horses away from Clem to give Tiny more room to swing his arm. Carl slides his rifle back into the scabbard but Rollo keeps his six-gun trained on Clem, letting him know that there is no escape.

'Now don't go drawing your gun,' Tiny tells Clem, 'because if Rollo has to shoot you that will take away all the fun.' He laughs, flicks his wrist but only slightly, just enough for the lash to snake across the ground, teasing Clem as to when the first real strike will be made.

A whip is a cruel weapon, not only because of the searing pain that each strike inflicts but because it debases a man. The scars remain for everyone to see. Clem knows only one tactic against a whip. He must get close to the man so that he cannot swing his arm, but he knows that won't be easy. Tiny Duggett looks like a man with previous experience of using a whip as a weapon and will be prepared for most manoeuvres. Furthermore, the two horsemen will undoubtedly intervene if he makes things difficult for Tiny.

Even so, Clem must try, must get to the man before he can stripe him. He sways backwards as though he intends running beyond the whip's range but springs forward, hoping he will get the first advantage. Tiny however, is prepared for such an opening. He moves quickly for a big man, bounding backwards, maintaining the gap. He chuckles and once more wiggles the lash across the ground, its movement reminiscent of a sidewinder snake.

His first manoeuvre thwarted, Clem keeps his eyes fixed on Tiny's face. Perhaps some tic, a twitch of the lips or a blink of the eyes will betray the launch of an assault. Carl Pelton mutters with impatience. 'Get on with it, Tiny. Someone might come along.'

'Got to enjoy it, Carl. Watch him sweat because he knows he can't get away. There's no escape for you, Rawlings. I'm going to slice you up real good.'

Clem believes him. If Tiny just sets to whipping him with all his strength then he has no hope of victory, but if Tiny becomes over confident, if he teases Clem at first with a few half-hearted lashes, then perhaps he'll be able to catch the whip and take it away from Tiny. But deep within he knows that Tiny is much stronger and has allies eager to cancel out any advantage he might gain.

Then it begins and any thoughts or plans Clem entertains for his survival are destroyed. Tiny heeds Carl's words because he is aware that this is no time to dawdle. He sweeps his arm and the lash flies through the air with a crack and curls around Clem's body. It slashes through his shirt, cuts a line across his back like a gash from a Bowie knife. Clem yells and he arches his back, all thought of trying to catch the lash in his hands is forgotten. His eyes are closed as he tries to absorb the pain when the next lash lands. This one is delivered with a more powerful arm movement. Again, it wraps around Clem, shreds his shirt and draws a spray of blood from his body. He staggers, almost falls, but determination keeps him upright.

Clem feels that the third blow has almost cut him in two. The lash completely encircles him and when Tiny yanks it free he succeeds in pulling Clem off his feet. Face down he is at Tiny's mercy, and Tiny has none. The pounding in Clem's ears almost obliterates other sounds but through the mist of pain he identifies Carl's voice urging Tiny on to greater effort. Three more lashes are delivered with immense power. Clem's shirt is now strips of rag and his back is a bloody mess. The pain is so intense that momentarily he loses consciousness.

When he regains his senses he realizes that Tiny is no longer using the whip. He doesn't know how many more strokes have been laid across his back but like all wounded animals he has sought protection by curling into a ball. Someone is tying a loop around his shoulders. The rubbing of the rough rope against the open wounds is an indescribable torment but then he is pulled along the ground behind a horse and as his lacerated body bounces across the dry earth he feels sure that he has reached the last inch of his life.

CHAPTER NINE

Being an ex-civil war soldier and a survivor of Shiloh, Rollo Wilson is not a stranger to blood and gore. He hired on with the Circle-E outfit to push cows and knows that he has only himself to blame for the fact that the job has drifted in another direction, but a man looks at the cards he's dealt and lays out his money accordingly. Now he has as much to lose as Tiny, Carl and everyone else mixed up in the enterprise, yet he has no taste for the needless punishment meted out to young Rawlings, and if killing him is the only solution then a bullet will do the job the same as it has done for Gus Farley. Not long ago they had been his bunkhouse pals and he had had no argument with either of them. Tiny, on the other hand, has allowed a taunt to develop into a scuffle, a scuffle into a rage and a rage into a blood-lust which he is satisfying with one ferocious lash after another. So, when Tiny Duggett puts aside his whip and Carl Pelton begins to drag young Clem Rawlings behind his horse, Rollo, having no wish to participate in the act of pulverizing a man to death, rides to the top of a small knoll and waits.

Carl Pelton's course is a large circle which he has three-quarters completed when Rollo espies the distant travellers. He yells a warning to Tiny and with a series of signals with his hat gets the message to Carl, too. Carl's immediate response is to release the rope that is cinched around his saddle horn and leave the body he has been dragging in a cloud of settling dust. Tiny and Rollo race for the tree cover from which they had earlier emerged and Carl, a quarter of a mile behind, chases after them.

It is the speed of their departure that attracts the attention of the people in the buggy whose curiosity is increased by the two loose horses that graze in the distance.

'Better take a look over there,' says Sepp Yates as he turns the vehicle towards the high ground, but it isn't until he's brought the team alongside that he recognizes the lump on the ground as the body of a man.

The clothes have been torn from his back and the angry, bloody weals are smothered with dust and earth. With care, Sepp raises the man's head, wondering if he is one of his own crew.

'Is he alive?' asks Joanna as she jumps out of the buggy. Her concern is apparent because, like her father, she feels sure that man will work on their ranch.

'Barely,' he says. 'Bring the water canteen.' He rests the man's head on his thighs so that he can identify him without the need of lying his ripped back on the ground. Joanna's shadow falls over him and they both recognize Clem Rawlings at the same moment.

'Let's get him in the buggy and back to the ranch,' says Sepp.

Joanna doesn't move. Her face wears a cold expression. The concern that filled her voice only moments before is gone and the canteen is gripped tightly in her hands as though she will defy all efforts to give succour to this man.

'Give me the water,' Sepp orders, although he understands the thoughts in his daughter's head. 'We can't leave him here to die. That would make us no better than the people who did this.'

Although it is not an instantaneous action, Joanna relinquishes the canteen and stands by while her father dashes some of its contents on to Clem's face.

The young man's eyes flicker open. His lips move. 'Gus,' he says.

Sepp raises his head and looks across the plain to the place where the two horses still graze. 'Gus Farley,' he murmurs and knowing that it is probable that Gus, too, is injured, he sends his daughter on to the ranch. 'Send someone back with a buckboard,' he tells her, 'and someone into town for the doctor. This boy needs urgent attention.'

Although she believes that she will always hate Clem Rawlings for his part in the lynching of Pat Baker, her father's few words have lodged in Joanna's mind. Seeking vengeance for the lynching by neglect makes her no better than the men who left him for dead, so she undertakes the ride to Enterprise herself and brings Doc Polworth back to the ranch. The physical demands of the journey coupled with its urgent purpose serve to distract her from the overpowering emptiness that has gripped her since Harv Golden broke the news of Pat's death. Later, despite herself, she waits with her mother to hear the doctor's verdict on Clem Rawlings's condition.

Doc Polworth can do little more for Clem's immediate comfort than has already been done by Joanna's mother. Susanna Yates has sluiced away the dust, grit and grime that might have infected the open wounds, then applied a concoction of egg white and lard to soothe and seal the gashes, treatment which earns the doctor's approval. He stays long enough to share ham, eggs and biscuits with the family, a meal which is guaranteed to bring him back for a look at the patient within a couple of days, and leaves behind a salve of turpentine, sweet oil and beeswax to be applied to Clem's back twice a day.

For two feverish days Clem Rawlings is confined to a cot in Sepp Yates's bunkhouse. With his back sliced and seared with whip lashes and his front scoured from being hauled behind a horse, every movement is torment.

When Clem finally regains a consciousness that is free of feverish frenzy he finds Gus Farley at his side. The older man's upper left arm is tightly bandaged and his face bears an abnormal grey tinge, but he smiles when the other's eyes focus on him.

'Where are we?' Clem asks.

'Sepp Yates's bunkhouse.'

Clem blinks; he's sure there's a reason for not being here but his brain can't quite sort out facts. 'What happened?'

'Tiny Duggett,' says Gus.

Instantly Clem remembers the bullwhip. He moves and instantly winces as he stretches the sealed slashes. 'I thought you were dead,' he tells Gus.

'Yeah. So did Sepp when he found me but this is only a scratch.' He indicates his arm. 'The major damage happened when I hit my head on the ground. Knocked myself unconscious.'

'You should have gone to Montana,' Clem tells his friend.

'I'll go when you go.'

Later, they are joined by Sepp Yates who, after remarking on the improvement of the health of both men, turns the conversation to the events on the night that Pat Baker died. Gus leaves nothing out of the account which includes their departure from the Circle-E and Nat Erdlatter's threat to have Clem whipped within an inch of his life.

'Pat was here,' Sepp confirms when Gus finishes his account.

'That's what we figured,' Gus tells him, 'but everything happened too fast for us to put up an argument.'

'And Nat Erdlatter wouldn't let him speak.' This is spoken ruminatively, not as a question. Sepp shakes his head as though it is the most unfair thing he's ever heard. Then he says, 'Sheriff Bright is in Enterprise. You'll tell him that?'

'We've spoken with Tyro Brooks,' Gus tells him.

'Did you tell him that Pat wasn't given a chance to defend himself?'

Gus shuffles, manipulating his wounded arm as though it is troubling him but it is nothing more than a tactic to give himself a moment to think. 'I've worked for Mr Erdlatter for a long time,' he begins, but Sepp Yates interrupts.

'And I've been his neighbour a long time, since before his boy and my girl were born. Ah hell, Gus, I understand loyalty and I'm not looking to have another neck stretched as revenge for what was done to Pat, but it was wrong and the only way to stop it happening again is to tell the truth and let the law take its course.'

Sepp Yates is a taciturn man and his last speech contains more words than either Clem or Gus have ever heard him utter at one time, but even though he is soft-spoken his words carry his anger and frustration. Clem suspects that there is also an element of fatherly care for his grieving daughter. The thought that this is Joanna's home unsettles Clem. Remembering how she, too, had been prepared to use a buggy whip on him presents an awkward situation.

'Perhaps we should return to Enterprise,' Clem suggests. 'I'm grateful for what you've done for me, Mr Yates, but I'll be fine now.'

Perhaps something in Clem's expression has betrayed his thoughts to Sepp because there is understanding in his eyes when he replies. 'You need to stay here a couple of days,' he says, 'give your back a chance to heal. Otherwise, if Tiny Duggett is still looking for you finishing you off will be an easy task.'

'My back is fine,' says Clem, which is a lie rebutted

each time he moves.

'Joanna brought the doctor,' Sepp tells him, so that his daughter's acceptance of the situation is understood. 'Her reaction when she saw you in Enterprise was that of any grieving woman who'd just learned of the unjust death of her man. Since then Harv Golden's spoken on your behalf and we've heard what you did for Josh Grant and his daughter. I'm not saying Joanna's forgotten you were at the hanging but her mind is open to the fact that you may not be as guilty as some of the other people who were there.'

Clem is still uneasy with the situation but he knows that staying with the Yates for two more days is a sensible decision.

The following morning Doc Polworth arrives to check on the progress of Clem and Gus and brings with him a surprise visitor. Lucy Grant, whom Clem had last seen stretched out unconscious on Drover Street, steps gracefully down from Doc's buggy, wearing a grey/blue travelling coat and matching hat. Over her arm she carries a cloth-covered basket.

'I hope my visit isn't an inconvenience,' she says to Mrs Yates, 'but when Doc told us of the injuries to Clem and Gus I insisted that he brought me along.'

'Come into the house,' invites Mrs Yates, 'while the doctor deals with his patients.'

Joanna is in the kitchen. 'Lucy is visiting Clem and Gus,' her mother tells her as the girls say Hello.

Lucy puts the basket on the table. 'Mother sent some bread and pies. She hopes it will help. She says

Gus alone can eat two steers a day.' She smiles, as does Mrs Yates.

Joanna speaks tartly. 'I'm sure we're able to feed our own guests.'

'Joanna!' exclaims her mother.

Lucy is taken aback. 'I didn't mean to imply otherwise. We wanted to let them know we were thinking about them. Food is our business, or it will be when we get new premises.'

'Where are you staying at the moment?' asks Mrs Yates, trying to steer the conversation in another direction.

'At Mrs Boswell's until the end of the week, but there are empty premises on Hill Street which will be suitable for a short while, until our own place has been rebuilt.' Joanna lets their conversation flow over her, she doesn't know why she is put out by Lucy Grant's visit.

Doctor Polworth is pleased enough with the progress of his patients. 'There are some deep lacerations across your back,' he tells Clem, 'so don't try to do too much too soon. You might find that they bleed or ooze pus if you put strain on your back before it's had time to heal. Keep the wounds clean and you should soon be back to normal.'

He tells them the news from town while examining Gus's wound. 'Tom Bright arrived yesterday and spoke with Harv Golden and some of the other settlers. He emphasized that he's come to sort out the matter according to the law and everyone will have to live with whatever conclusion he reaches. Of course Jim Welsh spoke out of turn, said that Tom would decide in favour of the cattlemen, which would give them free rein in future to do whatever they choose at the home-steaders' expense. Tom told Jim that if he carries on rabble-rousing he'll lock him away. Jim's response was that if that happens the homesteaders will nominate their own man to oppose him as sheriff and they might consider bringing in vigilante riders to protect their property.'

'What do you think will happen, Doc?' Gus asks.

'No idea. I don't risk predicting the weather in July,' he jokes, 'but I hope Tom Bright does act without bias otherwise me and the undertaker will be busy men. Jim Welsh might be a lone campaigner at the moment but he'll gain a lot of support for his views if the lynching is brushed under the carpet. If the homesteaders bring in vigilantes there'll be killings on both sides.'

They go across to the house and the tense atmos-phere there is apparent to all the men. Doc accepts a cup of coffee from Susanna Yates while Clem, Gus and Lucy find a place to sit outside.

'Tyro Brooks thinks the fire was started deliberately,' Lucy informs her saviours.

'Does he have any suspects?'

'No. Who would want to? Considering the way Pa is it would be a cowardly act.'

Gus and Clem exchange a look, both sharing the same thought that recently some riders of the Circle-E have been guilty of more than one cowardly act. Neither man gives voice to the thought but both wonder if the attack was provoked by the fact that they had been allowed to eat at the restaurant when the Circle-E men were banned.

When it is time to leave Joanna intercepts Lucy and takes her to one side.

'I was ill-mannered earlier,' she says. 'I don't know why. You didn't do anything to deserve that.'

'Three nights ago,' Lucy tells her, 'those men were very courageous. They entered an inferno to save not only my life but also my father's. The little bit of food I brought doesn't repay what we as a family owe, it is merely a gesture to show our gratitude. But perhaps that is what you took offence at, the fact that someone sees something admirable in those men at a time when such a thing is difficult for you. Only a few people know the truth of what happened when Pat Baker was killed and perhaps it will never be made known to the majority, but no matter what story is eventually broadcast I won't believe that Clem or Gus acted dishonourably.'

Joanna, stung by Lucy's defence of Gus and Clem, watches the buggy judder its way along the rutted road. When she turns she finds Clem some distance away also watching the buggy recede into the distance.

'You have an admirer,' she tells him. There is bitterness in her tone which she's not sure she intends but she can't prevent herself adding more. 'At least there'll be someone to mourn you when you're made to pay for Pat's murder.' She walks on, angry with herself, wishing she had more control of her emotions, wishing that the warmth of the day would rid her of the coldness she holds inside.

At the corner of the house, out of sight of Clem

Rawlings, she halts and raises the bottom of her apron to her eyes. There is a cough, a rough attempt at politeness. She uncovers her eyes and Gus Farley is leaning against the wall a mere handful of feet from her. She lets the apron fall back into place and smoothes it with her hands.

'Dust,' she says although the wetness of her eyes tells a different story.

He nods as though accepting the lie as truth. 'If you were less hard on the boy you might have less trouble with it,' he says.

Joanna's mouth opens as though a torrent of words is about to pour out but nothing comes. She lifts her skirts as if preparing to march on to the kitchen door but she doesn't take a solitary step. Her eyes remain fixed on Gus's face, knowing that he has more to say.

'Do you know why I quit riding for the Circle-E?' he asks, but the question is rhetorical because he's never explained his reason to anyone. 'It wasn't to ride clear of the territory because of what was done to Pat Baker, if that's what you think. No, I did it because of the courage and the honesty of that young fellow. He stood toe to toe with Nat Erdlatter and told him that what he'd done was wrong. It takes a courageous man to do that, but it was more than his words that got to me. He spoke up for Pat and defended him like a lioness with her cubs and I figured that if he would do that for someone who wasn't his friend then he was a man you'd be proud to ride with. I quit alongside Clem and we're heading for Montana together. He's a good man, Miss Yates, who has got himself mixed up in something that was none of his doing.'

'Pat Baker is still dead,' she says softly.

Gus nods. 'Nothing anyone can do about that now, but if there was then Clem Rawlings would be doing it. Believe me, your sharp words are minor wounds compared to those he is inflicting on himself. It was a bad thing that happened over on the south pasture, he knew it at the time and couldn't do anything to stop it.'

'Why weren't Pat and Clem friends?' she asks.

'Well, miss, I'm sure you know the answer to that yourself. They weren't enemies but they were rivals.'

Joanna lowers her head and heads indoors.

CHAPTER TEN

Lifting the saddle on to the horse's back proves to be a Herculean effort for Clem. By the time he has fastened the cinch he is exhausted. He rests his head against the grey's neck while he regathers his strength. He is sweating, in agony and fearful that he's torn open those healing lacerations that have so recently brought words of satisfaction from Doc Polworth, but getting away from the Tumbling-Y ranch, even for a short while, has become a necessity. Joanna's barely retained enmity is difficult to endure.

At the gate, Gus tries to intercept him.

'Where are you going?' he asks.

'Riding.'

'Let me get saddled up. I'll come with you,' Gus calls as his young comrade ups the pace to a canter.

Without reply, Clem rides west into the high ground, needing to be alone, needing to test himself, needing to prove that in the morning he'll be able to leave the Yates place for good. Perhaps he will take the advice of Gus and Fred Hardwick and ride fast for the border.

Hanging around Enterprise isn't likely to achieve any-thing except get him and Gus into more trouble. If there is going to be a war between the cattlemen and settlers he'll be as incapable of stopping it as he was of stopping Pat Baker's lynching. The best plan of action, he tells himself, is to keep his nose out of this Wyoming squabble and find a job pushing cattle in Montana.

However, once out of sight of the ranch house he cuts north, once again seeking the cattle trail that he and Gus had been following when the ambush had been sprung. Despite convincing himself that he should forget the events that have led to his current condition he finds it impossible to abandon them. He knows that there is only a slim possibility that Circle-E men are still on the lookout for him, the Erdlatters and their foreman will require their crew to earn their dollar a day in more productive fashion. In any case, Clem expects to cut the cattle trail further west than the ambush point, a point further away from the Erdlatter range.

After twenty minutes his search is rewarded although he is not sure that the trail he has come across is the same as the one that he and Gus followed a few days earlier. A closer examination proves that this trail is less than a day old and has been created by a smaller bunch of cattle, no more than a dozen, Clem reckons. Shod pony-prints are easy to spot and it is clear that these animals, like those that had created the earlier trail, are heading into the folds of the high ground.

In order to protect the healing processes at work on

his back, Clem has been riding with an unnatural posture, keeping himself straighter and stiller than usual. Now he arches his back, carefully, but winces as he experiences a searing pain. For a second it consumes his mind, biting so deeply that it is almost as though Tiny Duggett is once more behind him testing the strength of his arm. When the moment passes, when Clem has adopted a bearable position, he kicks on into the hills.

As he suspects, the trail among the gulches becomes more difficult to follow. The ground is too hard to show prints. He picks a route above the canyon floor, hoping to benefit from a bird's-eye view, and rides on for another hour.

Pulling the grey to a halt he scans the territory ahead. There is little of significance to see, no obvious sign that a bunch of cattle have been driven this way. A prominent crest about half a mile ahead seems a likely place to end his search. If that viewpoint fails to throw any light on the whereabouts of the chased cattle he'll return to the Tumbling-Y ranch.

Before him, when he sits at the edge of the crest, is a panorama of sky and hills. Somewhere beyond the high ground there are cattle ranches as large as the Circle-E or Tumbling-Y, but Clem dismisses the idea that those legitimate ranchers are involved in rustling cattle from this side of the hills. He knows that the town of Buffalo lies somewhere due west of where he sits and that south from there is the larger community of Casper with its rail spur to Cheyenne. It is difficult for rustlers to sell stolen cattle there because responsible railhead cattle

buyers deal with large herds and demand proof of own-
ership, preferably a registered brand for the territory, so
driving cattle through the hills to Casper seems
unlikely. Clem dismisses such an option from his mind.
He eases himself in the saddle once more, relaxes his
muscles until he receives a painful reminder of the
newly forming skin that is proud on his back.

Below him, the valley he has been following seems to
continue westerly, perhaps leading all the way to
Buffalo. The valley itself no longer has a river running
through it, but there is a pool which presumably is fed
from an underground source. A number of trees grow
close to the pool and their long shadows stretch like
fingers towards a narrow, north-bound pass among the
hills. For a moment Clem considers going down to
check for evidence of cattle movement, then something catches his eye. Among the trees two men sit
astride horses. They are waiting for something or
someone, then one of them raises his arm and signals
to Clem, beckoning him down to join them.

Clem is cautious lest they are Circle-E men inviting
him into another ambush. For a further moment he
remains motionless, watching the two men; then, sure
that he has never seen them before, begins a descent to
the valley floor.

It is clear as they watch his approach that the man
who signalled did so at the other's bidding. He is a
dusty traveller in grubby, worn clothing who sits his
horse like one accustomed to working in the saddle.
His companion wears a good quality corduroy jacket, a
brushed Stetson and his tough cord trousers disappear

into well-polished leather boots that reach almost to his knee. He sits erect, his right fist pressed against his right hip like one who is accustomed to issuing orders and having them obeyed. His pale blue eyes are unflinching and depict a man who will meet both pleasure and trouble head on. It is he who speaks first.

'I expected Mr Bell,' he says, wasting no time on introductions.

'You've got the wrong man,' Clem tells him, 'I don't know anyone called Bell.'

'Owner of the B-bar-B. Big spread hereabouts.'

Clem disagrees. 'You're in the wrong section, I reckon. Biggest spreads in these parts are the Circle-E and the Tumbling-Y.'

The dusty man removes a scrap of paper from his shirt pocket, examines it, gives a curt nod then hands it to the other. 'This is the spot,' he says. 'No mistake.'

The other man, the boss, barely glances at the paper before passing it on to Clem. 'Bob Bell,' he announces, as though speaking the name will produce the man and all misunderstanding will disappear, 'has five hundred head of cattle for sale. We agreed to meet here to complete the deal.'

'Looks like the right spot,' agrees Clem, passing back the sketched map, 'but all I've seen today is a handful of strays.'

'I need more than a handful, there are empty stock-yards at Casper that I mean to fill. I'm a cattle buyer,' the apparent boss explains. 'The name is Warren. Jim Warren and I'm paying top dollar for steers to ship east.'

'Doesn't look like that fellow Bell is coming,' says Warren's companion. 'No point hanging around here.'

Warren agrees although he is prepared to make camp for the night, willing to give the seller some leeway to allow for unexpected hazards while bringing the cattle through the hills. His man, Ben Gallon, argues against it.

'I recommend returning to Buffalo,' he says. 'You're not going to meet many ranchers up in these hills. If Bell still wants to deal he knows where to find you.'

It is sound advice and they ride away. Clem stays a moment, giving the grey an opportunity to drink from the pool and tossing over in his mind the coincidence of the bunch of cattle he's trailed from the south pasture with the missing herd that Jim Warren hopes to buy. His earlier thoughts about the need for documents when transporting steers by railroad come to mind but now the possibility of selling stolen cattle to a buyer nags at him. Perhaps it can be achieved by a clever and determined outlaw.

Behind him, from among a scattering of trees on the lower hump of the hill that he had descended to reach the pool, there is a noise. The grey raises his black head in sudden surprise. Clem turns in the saddle and grimaces as his movement causes a slash of pain across his back. Even so, and with his eyes almost closed as he grits his teeth against the pain, he realizes that someone has stepped out from the trees with a rifle in his hands. He raises it, aims at Clem and fires.

Despite the painful handicap of his lacerated back, Clem reacts instantly, throwing himself forward along his horse's neck. The bullet misses him by inches, passing over his back to sing away over the pool. Clem clings to the horse, turns it away from the pool with the intention of riding out of range of his attacker, but another shot is fired and it is quickly followed by a third.

The second shot passes in front of the grey, close to its head, spooking it, causing it to rear. Clem slips, the sudden movements of his mount bringing sheets of agony to his back. Mechanically, he grabs his rifle and when another bullet passes close to his body he is left with no alternative other than to dismount so that the horse is between himself and the gunman. A nearby low mound offers some protection, and while the grey is still in the gunman's line of fire Clem scampers towards it.

Earth kicks up near his hands and legs as Clem scrambles the last three or four yards. He spreads full length on the ground behind the mound, the shape providing a natural fortification so that he is instantly able to return fire. His shots fly in the general direction of the gunman so that he, too, is forced to take cover and for a few moments there is silence. The smell of gunpowder lingers in the air. Clem raises his head slightly to look for the shooter but cannot spot him.

Suddenly, a bullet smacks the ground near his head. As dirt and grass shoot up and strike his face he is conscious of the fact that the shot has been fired from an unexpected point. Other shots follow. As he throws himself to the side to avoid them he realizes that he is caught in a cross-fire. Immediately, he comes under fire from the first shooter and bullets kick and ricochet around him.

Ignoring the pain in his back he lifts his head, hoping to return fire, but they have him too well pinned down and more shots rain down around his position. Movement to either side is impossible for him without being hit. The man to his right shouts to the first shooter, who is now among the trees.

'I'll keep him pinned down. Move around and finish him.'

Clem suspects that this may be a ruse to make him concentrate on the man to his left and that it will be the man to his right who advances, but he draws shots every time he raises his head and he has no idea how the duo's attack is developing. It is suicide, however, for him to wait for their plan to unfold so, with no option remaining, he wriggles, snakelike, backwards towards the edge of the pool.

Behind the mound the land slips away in a short, grassy stretch, then drops suddenly, four or five feet to the lip of the pool. Because it is downhill, Clem hopes that the mound keeps his movement obscured from his attackers. However he knows that every moment could be his last, that already they have him in their sights and are waiting for the cleanest shot. He moves slowly, squirming inch by inch back towards the lip of the pool, holding his rifle at the ready, keeping his eyes fixed on the top of the mound for the appearance of a hat, a head, a gun or anything that tells him that his unknown enemies are upon him.

Due to the tension of the situation, Clem miscalculates

the distance he must cover. Sooner than expected he reaches the lip of the pool and finds himself toppling down the short embankment. He cries out, partly because of the surprise but mainly because in attempting to prevent himself falling he has twisted and his back bears the brunt of the impact.

At that moment and despite his agony, he is aware of two events. The first, and most immediate to be dealt with, is the appearance of a man to the left of the mound, a man whose face wears a startled expression, registering his surprise that Clem's shout has come from a point beyond where he expects him to be. The man reacts quickly, swinging his rifle towards Clem and firing instantly. The shot is hurried, the aim poor and the bullet misses. The man ratchets the mechanism of the Winchester but his second shot is poorer than the first, digging a hole in the ground three inches in front of his own right boot. The reason is that Clem, half in the water, has returned fire, half a second behind the rustler's shot but with greater accuracy. His bullet has hit his assailant in the stomach, causing him to fold and fire his second shot as his knees buckle. He pitches forward on to his face.

The second event that registers with Clem is the sound of hoofbeats. Believing that it is the other man riding away he scurries awkwardly up the bank, but discovers that Jim Warren and Ben Gallon have returned to investigate the shooting.

The other shooter has made his escape, sacrificing his companion in the face of Clem's reinforcements. Neither Jim nor Ben saw the man but both recognize

111

the dead one lying dead at Clem's feet.

'He was in Buffalo when we spoke with Bob Bell,' says Ben Gallon. 'They were drinking whiskey at the bar together when we arrived.'

Jim Warren agrees and Clem, too, has seen the man before.

'Came looking for work at the Circle-E,' he says. 'Two of them, but Mr Erdlatter said he had hands enough. They rode on.'

'Why are they hunting you?' asks Jim Warren.

'Because I'm trailing stolen cattle,' Clem tells him. His face and voice are now unable to disguise his pain. 'Possibly the same cattle that you're out here to buy.'

Jim Warren is curious about that remark but he sees the blood on Clem's back and decides his questions will have to wait. Convinced that Clem will not be able to protect himself in the event of another attack, Jim and Ben ride with him back to the Tumbling-Y.

CHAPTER ELEVEN

At the ranch, while Jim Warren and Ben Gallon give an account of the gunfight in the hills, Susanna Yates insists on tending to the reopened lacerations across Clem's back. More than one tut escapes her lips as she works, bathing away the dried blood then coating the open wounds with the doctor's ointment. It stings Clem like the bites of a thousand rattlesnakes, leaving him nauseated and barely able to swallow more than a couple of spoonfuls of the stew that is put before him.

Gus Farley's criticism that riding out alone had been a reckless act only rubs salt in Clem's wounds. He'd known when he left the Tumbling-Y that afternoon that, in the event of running into members of Erdlatter's crew, he was barely capable of defending himself. Gus, he knows, is more of a friend than he currently deserves, and by ignoring his advice he is being made to pay for Joanna's goading.

Bunks are found for Jim Warren and Ben Gallon but before they put them to use they join Clem, Gus and the Yates family to discuss the situation. Neither Sepp

Yates nor Gus know a rancher called Bob Bell, nor do they recognize the brand described by the cattle-buyer; two Circle-Bs joined by a bar. But Jim Warren's description of the man with whom he'd hoped to do business make his identity clear. 'A big man with red hair,' he declares, 'carries a scar from the corner of his left eye to the centre of his cheek.'

'Jos Hammond,' Gus mutters. He, Clem and Sepp exchange glances that ask why the foreman of the Circle-E should be involved in the sale of cattle which bear another brand.

Clem offers up his theory that rustled cattle are being rebranded and held somewhere in the hills before being trailed west through the narrow valleys to the stockyards at Casper.

'Bills of sale in favour of the new brand will make their transport East a legitimate act,' he declares.

Sepp Yates shakes his head, full of doubt that such a scheme could be successful, but after admitting that he's been losing cattle over recent weeks he gives the matter more consideration.

Jim Warren assures him that determined men will always find a way to sell on stolen cattle. 'It could work,' he tells those assembled, 'I've heard of similar schemes in the cow towns of Arizona.'

Gus scratches his jaw. 'Are you saying that Red Hammond is one of the rustlers?' he asks Clem.

Clem nods.

Until this moment Joanna Yates has been silent, offering neither words of concern to Clem nor assistance to her mother's nursing care, but now, with the implication that Nat Erdlatter's top hand is guilty of the rustling of which he'd accused Pat Baker, the colour leaves her face. She rises, goes into the kitchen so that her distress is hidden from the rest of the people present.

'What do we do now?' Gus wants to know.

'Let Tom Bright handle it,' says Sepp Yates. 'I got word that his enquiries will bring him here tomorrow.'

Clem's response is terse. 'Tom Bright won't hunt hidden steers. We'll have to find them and lead him to them.'

'He'll listen to Jim,' argues Sepp, pointing at the cattle-buyer and earnestly believing that the sheriff will act on Jim Warren's evidence. 'That will lead to the arrest of Jos Hammond and everyone else involved.'

Clem wants to argue; his face betrays the fact that Tom Bright is likely to report to Nat Erdlatter before taking any decisive action, and that by showing his hand there is a risk that Red Hammond will be given the chance to take flight.

As though reading his companion's mind, Gus speaks. 'Erdlatter's losing stock, too. If Red's involved he'll be made to pay.'

Joanna has returned to the room; she is carrying a full coffee pot as though refilling cups had been her reason for going to the kitchen. 'Clem is right,' she says. 'Sheriff Bright will only act if we have indisputable evidence. Look what happened today.'

Sepp Yates nods, accepting his daughter's verdict. Clem looks from one to the other for an explanation. 'What happened?' he finally asks.

'Jim Welsh has been locked up,' Gus tells him. 'There was an incident in Enterprise.'

'I don't think it was too serious,' Sepp offers.

'No one was hurt,' says Gus, 'but guns were fired. Jim Welsh and Dusty Thoms got into an argument.'

'But only Jim Welsh is in Tyro Brooks's jail house,' says Joanna, a statement which carries the weight of her conviction that the Erdlatters are not subject to any law.

'Jim Welsh,' her father says, 'is a hot-head.'

'He has reason to be,' says his wife. 'Poor man. If Nat Erdlatter's men hadn't destroyed that bridge then the doctor might have reached his wife.'

The incident had happened before Clem Rawlings had arrived in the territory but he'd often heard it spoken of. Some of Nat Erdlatter's crew had destroyed a new bridge over the Westwater as part of their campaign to drive away the settlers. Jim Welsh was one of those who had chosen land on the south side of the river and when the floods came he was cut off from Enterprise and the doctor wasn't able to reach his wife during childbirth. Both she and the baby died but there was no law that Jim could call upon for retribution; all he was left with was an emptiness in his life and a desire that one day Nat Erdlatter would be made to pay.

'What will happen to Jim Welsh?' asks Clem.

'A night in the cells, perhaps a fine and a warning as to his future behaviour.'

'And Dusty Thoms?'

'He's back at the Circle-E. Erdlatter promised to

116

keep him on the ranch. Jim Welsh was lucky he picked on Thoms; some of the other hands are more deadly with their six-guns.'

Without a clear course of action decided, they go to their beds.

Next morning, Jim Warren declares that other cattle buyers will acquire all the herds if he's not in Buffalo by evening so, despite Sepp Yates's attempt to keep him at the Tumbling-Y until the sheriff arrives, he and Ben Gallon make tracks after breakfast.

'If the sheriff requires statements from us we'll be either in Buffalo or around the Casper cattle pens,' he tells the rancher.

The assurance is less than Sepp has hoped for but because the cattle-buyer has already gone out of his way to escort Clem Rawlings back to the ranch he can't insist upon more. Tom Bright, however, has a reputation for being less than thorough in his endeavours to catch law-breakers, so Sepp fears that any testimony that Jim Warren and Ben Gallon can supply will never be given.

Although there are business deals awaiting completion in Buffalo, Jim Warren's decision to leave the ranch is purely personal. Involvement with law-officers is something he chooses to avoid. When he'd told Sepp Yates that determined men found ways to sell stolen cattle he failed to mention that he figured in some of those deals, consequently he gives sheriffs little encouragement to delve into his business. Clem Rawlings survived the attempted ambush, so he suspects there will be little effort on the part of Sheriff Bright or any other lawman to pursue the men involved. He rides away quite confident that he will hear nothing more of the matter.

A man watches as they approach the pool which had been yesterday's rendezvous point. He stands as they grow closer and removes his hat, thereby revealing his red hair.

'Mr Bell,' calls Jim Warren, 'our appointment was yesterday.'

Red Hammond offers up an excuse in which Jim Warren only pretends interest.

'Have you got my five hundred head?' he asks.

'Haven't cut them all out yet,' says Red.

'I heard you were gathering your herd bunch by bunch,' Warren tells him.

Red Hammond throws back his shoulders, faces up to Jim Warren, asks 'What do you mean by that?' although the cattle-buyer's implication is plain enough.

'Come, Mr Hammond,' says Warren, 'it is Mr Hammond, isn't it?' The scowl that settles on Red's face confirms that Warren has spoken the foreman's real name. 'I'm always suspicious of unregistered brands.'

'Who told you my name?'

'Does it matter? The important thing for you to know is that the law is closing in on you. Probably isn't safe for you to return to the Circle-E. Yes, I know what outfit you ride for. Top hand, I believe.'

Red's scowl deepens as he recognizes a threat in the

other's words. His hand strays towards the butt of his pistol but Ben Gallon's cough attracts his attention. Ben has unsheathed his rifle, holds it in a casual fashion, but the barrel is pointing at Red's stomach.

'No need for any unpleasantness,' says Jim Warren, 'I might still be in a position to take your herd.'

Red drags his attention away from the weapon that threatens him and inclines his head to let Warren know that he is listening.

'A drive to the Casper rail pens sets out tomorrow. If you push your cattle south west from here you'll intercept them in a day or two. I'll tell the trail boss to expect you. There's a whole mix of brands in the herds so your steers won't attract any attention.'

'What about my money?'

'Well, I'm not carrying that sort of money at the moment,' says Warren, tapping at his jacket as if to show that his pockets are empty, 'but I'll give the trail boss a wallet for you.'

Red Hammond can't shake free of the feeling that Warren has some other motive for offering to take the cattle; his distrust is evident in his tone when he asks, 'Why are you doing this?'

'Business is business'

'And I'll get cash?'

'Of course.'

'Forty dollars a head, as agreed?'

Warren laughs. 'Come, Mr Hammond, you can't expect top price for cattle that aren't your own. No, I was thinking fifteen dollars.'

'Fifteen?'

'You don't really have another option. You can't go back to Enterprise, I understand you had some part in having an innocent man lynched. And you can't find another buyer in Buffalo because I have a feeling that the Cattlemen's Association will learn of your presence in the area if you try that. So it's seven and a half thousand dollars or nothing. The choice is yours.'

Red Hammond seethes but he knows that Jim Warren has the upper hand. He also knows that, at present, he is well short of the agreed 500 head. Tonight there will be one last snatch of cattle from the range; then, before morning, they will drive the full herd out of the hills towards Casper.

Clem sits on a bench outside the kitchen. His back smarts and even though yesterday's incident hasn't added to the damage it has certainly slowed the healing process. His mind is on the cattle in the hills. If they can be found and the rustlers arrested it might put an end to the trouble that is brewing in Enterprise.

From time to time, however, those thoughts are interrupted. Sometimes it is Joanna Yates who fills his head, perplexed by her behaviour the previous night, supporting his argument though without any show of friendliness, barely casting a look in his direction. But Pat Baker, too, haunts him, a memory of that last lingering look before his body turned away on the end of the rope. If Red Hammond is involved with rustling cattle then Pat's death is an act of murder.

From the front of the ranch the rattle of the shutter door followed by the hollow sound of heeled boots on porch planks reaches Clem. He recognizes the gait of Sepp Yates but the footsteps stop and the rancher doesn't appear. Clem peers around the corner of the house. Sepp stands at the top of the steps that lead down to the yard. He doesn't see Clem, his gaze is fixed on a point beyond the yard gate where a rider is approaching at a determined canter. Clem assumes that this will be the expected visit from Sheriff Bright, but as the gap between rider and ranch house shortens he knows he is in error. The familiar stiff-backed riding and the big chestnut gelding both belong to Nat Erdlatter. Keeping out of sight, Clem leans a shoulder against the side of the house.

Nat Erdlatter rides through the gate and halts half a dozen paces from the porch.

'Sepp,' he says in greeting and begins to swing a leg over the gelding to dismount.

'Don't get down, Nat,' Sepp Yates tells him.

Erdlatter pauses, then settles back in the saddle. 'Something wrong?'

'This isn't time for visiting. If you've got some business here then state it.'

Erdlatter wears a puzzled expression. 'Never needed a reason to call by before, Sepp. We've been neighbours for a number of years.'

'We're still neighbours, Nat, but what happened the other night doesn't sit easy with this family. Hanging Pat Baker put a fence between us that's too high to see over.'

'Bah!' Erdlatter is dismissive of Sepp's remark. 'He was a cattle rustler, Sepp. Isn't that the punishment we've always dealt to that kind?'

'Twenty years ago, Nat, when there wasn't any other way. That was when we fought the gangs that came to drive off the small herds that were all that stood between us and starvation. But this was one boy, Nat, one boy who'd been in this ranch house not twenty minutes before you strung him up.'

'Here?'

'He was sparkin' my girl. They were serious, I guess. She's taken it bad.'

'Your girl, Sepp. Is that what this is all about?' He indicates himself still astride the horse, not invited into the house. 'Heck, she'll get over it. Girls change their minds about young fellas every new moon. Joanna's a good-looking girl, she'll find another beau soon enough. Why, she could marry my boy. Think of that Sepp, think of the size of range they would control some day.' He laughs, slaps his thigh as though he's found the most perfect solution.

Sepp doesn't share Erdlatter's joy. He hopes Joanna does soon find someone else, but not Vinny Erdlatter.

Erdlatter is talking again, his tone serious as though what has gone before has been brushed away by his vision of a united Erdlatter-Yates ranch. 'We've got trouble with those nesters,' he says, 'they want a trial and Tom Bright is making noises like he supports them. Tom Bright! I told him he's only sheriff of this county because I put him there.'

'Because the cattlemen supported him,' Sepp says.

Nat Erdlatter frowns, unable to distinguish the difference. 'Issuing orders as though he has some authority over me,' he continues, 'telling me to keep Dusty Thoms on the ranch until he's finished his investigation. If that Jim Welsh wasn't such a hot-head I doubt if the other nesters would be showing any interest at all.'

'You're wrong,' Sepp tells him, 'Pat Baker was well liked around Enterprise. Most people think that hanging him was unjust. As for Jim Welsh, it's a pity he hasn't found another woman to help soothe away his cares.'

Erdlatter shifts in the saddle, grunts out a note of derision. 'Lost my wife all those years ago. I don't sniffle about it, just got on with the business of building my ranch.'

'You seem to be forgetting how it was, Nat. After that raid you declared you'd kill every Cheyenne, man, woman and child and when they came a-raiding again you gave it a durned good try.'

Erdlatter sits motionless wearing his usual poker-face expression.

Sepp Yates continues: 'Jim Welsh hasn't had any such opportunity to purge himself for the loss of his wife. The needlessness of that death drags through his life like a plough on a rocky slope. It's no wonder that he rises like a salmon every time the farmers believe they have a grievance against the cattlemen.'

'A grievance against me, you mean. Well, if he was any kind of man he'd strap on a gun and come looking for me.'

Sepp shakes his head. 'He'd never get near you and you know it. Some of your men would be only too pleased to slap leather against a greenhorn farmer.

That's all that Jim Welsh is, Nat, a greenhorn farmer. He might shout a good fight but he has as much idea about gunfighting as I have about vine growing.'

'Then he should leave this territory. This is for cattlemen who fight for what they want.'

'You just don't see it, Nat. Times are changing. The people along the Westwater have been encouraged to settle there by the government. Stands to reason that the government will protect them with laws. Law officers like Tom Bright will have to enforce those laws if they want to stay in their job.'

Nat Erdlatter shows defiance. 'Tom Bright will do what the cattlemen tell him to do.'

'Could be you're right, Nat, just don't make the mistake of thinking that you speak for all the cattlemen. A range war won't profit any of them. Nobody wants to send out riders that could be shot out of their saddle for no good reason.'

'No good reason? What about the cattle that have been stolen? You've lost some, haven't you?'

'Sure, but I don't think the homesteaders are to blame. So if you came here to recruit my crew to frighten the homesteaders out of the territory you're going to leave a disappointed man.'

'Are you siding against me with those nesters?'

'We've got to face up to the fact that those people have a right to settle here. I reckon there's land enough for all of us.'

'Always thought you had more guts, Sepp.' Nat Erdlatter pulls on the reins to turn his horse and spurs it out of the yard.

124

When he hears Sepp's footsteps recross the porch and the shutter door swing closed, Clem lets out a sigh. He pushes himself away from the wall and turns to head towards the bunkhouse. Joanna is behind him. He has no idea how long she's been there.

'Eavesdropping?' she asks without humour.

'I thought it was the sheriff,' explains Clem. 'When I realized it was Mr Erdlatter I figured he wouldn't be pleased if he knew I was here. So I kept quiet. I didn't want to embarrass your father.'

For a moment they look at each other, keeping a silence that neither seems comfortable with but that neither seems to know how to break. Clem moves as though to pass the girl.

'How is your back?' she asks, the first time she has shown any concern for his injuries.

'Sore,' he says truthfully, 'but no worse than it was yesterday,' which is a lie.

'Mother will put more ointment on when you need it. It'll keep the wounds clean and ease the pain.'

'I won't be around,' he says.

'Where are you going?'

'To find the rustled cattle. I've an idea where they are.'

'You can't go alone,' she tells him. Her eyes darken as she remembers the injuries he's already suffered. 'You're hardly in condition to ride a horse.'

'I'll be OK,' he says. 'Gus will be with me.' The concern that shows in Joanna's eyes is fleeting but it is a genuine emotion and does more to lift Clem's spirit than all the potions in Doc Polworth's surgery. He knows it doesn't signify forgiveness for what happened on the south meadow but it is, at least, a beginning.

'Be careful,' the girl says, then turns to go back to the kitchen.

'Joanna,' he says, 'there's something I need to tell you.' She stops and turns back. 'It's about Pat.' He hurries his words to prevent her interrupting. 'I saw his face that night. The look he gave me has haunted me ever since. It's taken until now for me to make sense of it. I think he was trying to tell me something, trying to pass a message to me although he couldn't speak. I think he wanted me to tell you that at the very end, when he knew all hope was gone, he was thinking of you.'

CHAPTER TWELVE

Red Hammond's horse struggles to cover the final few steps of the steep, rocky slope then snorts dusty air from its nostrils when the climb is completed. Behind, Carl Pelton's saddle-horse, more suited to demonstrating the agile twists and turns of a working cow pony, stands on trembling legs, grateful for the respite after the long, arduous climb. On their backs, the riders scan the terrain below, sharp eyes seeking the movement that will confirm the effort has been worthwhile. It is Carl who stretches out an arm, pointing at the two horsemen they seek.

'Fifteen dollars a head,' murmurs Red. 'Let's see if we can negotiate a better price.' He taps the flanks of his horse, uncaring of its tiredness, proud of his own achievement that by crossing the high hill, he'd been able to cancel out the thirty minute advantage he'd allowed the cattle buyer.

For the first hour after parting from Red Hammond Jim Warren and Ben Gallon have kept a careful eye on their back trail, expecting at every moment to see some sign of pursuit. Now, almost out of the difficult hill country, thoughts of Red Hammond are at the back of their minds and their conversation concentrates on the cattle-drive from Buffalo to Casper, which will set out next day. When they come out of a turn in the trail it takes several moments before they recognize the rider who blocks their advance. Their surprise is evident as they pull hard on the reins and bring their horses to a halt. Even though a smile shows on Red's face they have no doubt as to his purpose.

Ten feet separate them when Red speaks. 'I'm asking forty dollars a head for my cattle,' he says.

Ben Gallon lets his hand slide to the stock of his rifle which is sheathed beneath his right leg.

Behind him, Carl Pelton speaks. 'I wouldn't touch that.' He moves on to the trail so that when Ben and Jim glance behind they see the pair of cocked pistols that are aimed in their direction.

Red Hammond's smile broadens. 'And just so that there aren't any further attempts to change the price I'll take the money now.'

In a show of bravado Jim Warren slaps at his jacket and says he has no money with him. 'I told you that earlier, Red.'

'But that was a lie, Jim. You came out from Buffalo with the specific purpose of buying five hundred head from me. You've got the money. Now throw your wallet over here.'

Jim looks once more at Carl Pelton, shrugs, as if admitting defeat and reaches into his jacket.

'Carefully,' orders Red.

Jim Warren holds a black wallet by a corner with the tips of his fingers, then settles it fully in his left hand as he prepares to throw it towards Red Hammond. With a flick of the wrist the thick billfold sails through the air and Red watches as it describes an arc which will carry it into his hands. Suddenly he realizes that Jim Warren's left hand isn't empty, a double-barrelled derringer sits snugly there and it is spouting flame in his direction before the wallet has covered half the distance between them.

Fortunately for Red, even at such a short distance the accuracy of the small gun is unreliable. The bullet tugs at his shirtsleeve. Instantly he draws his Colt and fires, his shot hitting Jim Warren in the heart. Simultaneously, Carl Pelton discharges both of his pistols and a second bullet hits Jim Warren in the back. Ben Gallon, too, is shot in the back and dies seconds after hitting the ground.

While Red retrieves the wallet and counts the money, Carl drags the bodies into nearby foliage, out of sight of the trail. With $20,000 in his pocket Red considers abandoning the stolen cattle and heading south to the safety of another state, but the lure of another $20,000 from selling the cattle at Casper is too great to ignore.

Confident that they can be clear of the territory before the law catches up with them, he and Carl head back towards Enterprise for one more rustling raid before driving the herd overnight to the railhead cattle pens.

*

Far from being deterred by the previous day's attempted ambush, Clem is eager to repeat his scouting expedition. He has concluded that his attackers could only have come from the shaded narrow valley he had observed from the crest above the pool, because he had seen no other riders during his careful inspection of the surrounding territory. That they had waited until he was alone before opening fire on him could have been a continuance of the Circle-E's campaign against him, but he was more apt to think that it was to avoid drawing Jim Warren and Ben Gallon into the affair. They were going to buy cattle so they wouldn't want them harmed.

It is late afternoon when Clem's hunch proves to be well-founded. The smell of cattle reaches him and Gus before they've ridden far into the high-walled valley. Splatters of dung as recent as two-days-old litter the valley floor and an occasional shod-hoofprint provides confirmation that these aren't beasts that have strayed in search of grass. The first lowing sound carries like a faint echo from some unseen locale ahead.

'We'll picket the horses among those pines,' Gus suggests, adding. 'No point announcing our presence until we know who and how many we're dealing with.'

Clem has no argument and after securing their mounts out of sight of the trail they go forward on foot, climbing the wall of rock to their right, not only to avoid a direct approach but also to find a place where they can observe without being seen.

The cattle are grazing at the head of the valley, a plateau-like area that forms a natural corral from

which there is no other egress. Water tumbles down
the far hillside and runs for a stretch of fifty yards
before disappearing, presumably into the underground cavern that supplies the pool at the mouth of
the valley. Gus estimates the herd at 300 head, signifi-
cantly lower than the figure that had been quoted to
Jim Warren, but neither he nor Clem have any doubt
that this is the herd that Jos 'Red' Hammond, aka Bob
Bell, proposes to sell to the cattle buyer. He nudges
Clem and points to the far side of the valley, where two
men are sitting on the ground. Though it is hard to distinguish their features it is clear that they are relaxed,
playing a card game, taking little interest in the docile
beasts they are there to guard.

'Recognize them?' asks Gus.

'One of them is Grat Todd,' answers Clem, 'and the
other came looking for work at the Circle-E a few days
ago, along with the man I killed yesterday.'

'I remember him,' mutters Clem. 'Guess somebody
hired him to rustle cattle.'

They both suspect that somebody to be Red
Hammond but neither speaks the name.

'What do we do now?' asks Gus.

'Bring Sheriff Bright out here. Let him make some
arrests and hope that it helps to calm matters back in
Enterprise.'

Gus rubs his jaw. 'Don't see how arresting Grat Todd
will ease the situation. That'll just prove Pat Baker was
innocent, which'll further rile the homesteaders.'

'Perhaps you're right,' concedes Clem, 'but there'll
be no peace until we get the truth sorted out.'

For a few minutes they sit in silence watching the peaceful scene below; lazy cattle and carefree men.

'I'd like to take a closer look at those steers,' says Clem. 'Need to check the brand to make sure that this is the herd that was offered to Jim Warren.'

'Too risky,' Gus tells him. 'Grat Todd might not be the best cowhand in Wyoming but he handles a rifle well enough. If he sees you he won't hesitate to prove it.'

Clem looks at the sky. 'The sun will be gone in a couple of hours,' he declares. 'I'll go down then.'

Putting stress on the first word to emphasize that he will brook no argument, Gus says, '*We*'ll go down then.'

There is little activity from below while they wait. The card game is interrupted only long enough for Grat to brew coffee and for his companion to lead their horses to the running water, and as the day darkens they move closer to the fire's glow so that they can continue their game.

The valley at twilight is a dark place, abounding in strange shadow shapes and fidgety noises which, without better explanation, are generally attributed to the breeze or roaming, unseen creatures. With the aid of this camouflage Clem leads the way downhill from their observation point. They move gingerly, determined not to alarm the cattle herders below. From the cover of one rock to another they descend, throwing the occasional glance in the direction of the small campfire, assuring themselves that the two men have not moved.

Soon they are among the steers, crouching low so

that they don't show above the animals' backs. The cattle shuffle around but are accustomed to the presence of men and make little fuss. Clem checks the brand on the nearest animal. It is the one described by Jim Warren, two Circle-Bs connected by a bar, cleanly burned above the left hind haunch. A quick inspection confirms that the nearest half a dozen animals are similarly marked.

Gus calls with a low voice. 'Look at this.' He is pushing at the rump of one steer so that Clem can approach. The animal grumbles, raises its head and bellows at the night sky. His neighbour is disturbed and answers with a call of his own. The two cattle shuffle, causing those close by to mill around and Clem and Gus have to move with them to avoid being squashed.

Gus indicates the brand that has been applied to the beast he's stuck close to. It is at an irregular angle, as though applied hurriedly or without care. However, it is not the manner of branding that has caught the attention of the older man but the top B, which is blurred as though the iron shifted in the brander's hand.

'See,' he points at the rest of the brand, 'all clean lines. If it was a bad branding then everything would be blurred.'

Clem knows what has happened; he's already tracing the under-mark with a finger. 'That's a Tumbling-Y underneath,' he says. 'Likely we'll find others.'

Gus nods. 'Majority of the herd are mavericks that have been rounded up and branded, but it looks like they've had to over-brand a few to increase the size of the herd.'

'Keep looking,' insists Clem. 'To make Nat Erdlatter accept that Pat Baker was innocent we need to prove that his own men were rustling his stock.'

They search for several minutes, taking care not to cause too much disturbance to the herd. They know that, with careful over-branding, changing an E to a B is difficult to detect but eventually they are rewarded. Even in the darkness of evening they can see the bungled attempt to over-brand a couple of steers.

'A close inspection in daylight will identify others,' Gus mutters. 'We should get out of here now.'

Clem agrees and wends a way among the sleepy beasts which, although reluctant to move, are prone to making sudden head movements with horns that are capable of delivering a deadly blow. Perhaps concentrating on that physical danger has momentarily wiped all other sources of danger from his mind but as he steps clear of the herd he hears a surprised shout some distance to his left.

'Hey,' the man yells. It is Grat Todd who, having become aware of the unrest among the distant cattle, has ridden around the herd to investigate. Suspecting that they have been spooked by a mountain cat he has his rifle unsheathed and lying across his knees. The sight of a man emerging from among the cattle takes him completely by surprise.

'Hey,' he yells again, raising the weapon so that the stock rests on his thigh and the barrel points at the sky.

Clem curses, stoops low and heads for the dark shadows of the hillside, gambling that Grat will not fire, will not risk startling the cattle with a gunshot. This sudden, necessary activity provokes a painful reminder that his back wounds are still in the process of healing. The lash cuts sting as he rushes forward, hoping to gain the protection of the first boulders before Grat is upon him. Behind, he can hear the sounds of pursuit, Grat's shouted warning and the quickening of the horse's hoofs.

Surprisingly, a shot rings out and a bullet zings close to his head, then strikes rock to ricochet away into the darkness. The cattle are moving and low their concern to each other. Clem runs on, weaving from side to side, presenting an even more difficult target in the darkness. Another shot is fired which strikes the ground a little to his left and he stumbles.

The thought is in his mind to draw his own gun but he is falling and stretches his arms to lessen the impact against the ground. He grunts, rolls on to his back and grimaces because the scars feel like embedded barbed wire. But concern for his discomfort is only momentary. Twenty yards away and closing the gap between them quickly is Grat Todd. His rifle is at his shoulder and he fires as Clem sprawls on the ground. That bullet misses and kicks up dirt near Clem's head. The next, he is sure, will not miss.

Before Grat can fire again another gun, somewhere behind the rider, is discharged. The horse squeals and rises on its hind legs. Unprepared, Grat slides off its back and lands hard and awkwardly on the dry ground. Under the sound of the pained horse and cursing rider Clem recognizes the scratchy clattering sound as the rifle slides across the rough ground. Grat, he knows, is also armed with a pistol and will be prepared to use it. Once again, Clem considers drawing his own weapon to put an end to the fight but he is reluctant to do so, preferring to have the sheriff arrest all the rustlers and discover the truth behind the hanging of Pat Baker.

Grat is struggling on to his knees, his hand is reaching for his pistol giving Clem no option but to reach for his own revolver. The need to draw it, however, is removed when Gus looms into sight and swipes his own gun across Grat Todd's head. The dull, heavy sound of the blow carries to Clem. Senseless, the rustler slumps into an untidy heap.

'Come on,' says Gus, pleased to see that his companion has not been hit by any of Grat's bullets, 'that other fellow is on his way. We've got to get back to the horses.'

Free for the moment of the need for secrecy, Clem and Gus head back along the valley floor to where they'd picketed their horses. Clem thinks it is possible that they might be pursued by Grat and his gambling companion. Gus allays his fears.

'When he comes round Grat Todd won't be eager to climb back on a horse. I hit him as hard as I could.'

Recalling the sound made when Gus's pistol and Grat's head collided forces Clem to agree. Still, he urges Gus to hurry. It might be some time before the two rustlers decide upon pursuit but he is sure it will come and by then he wants to be as far as possible away from this valley. It will be late when they reach Enterprise but if they speak to Sheriff Bright tonight he will be able to organize a posse for an early start in the morning. Estimating that they are three-quarters of a mile from the spot where they left their horses, they hurry on.

They are approaching a dogleg in the canyon, beyond which their horses are tethered and here, simultaneously, they stop, both troubled by the same sense of unease. The noise of cattle has stayed with them since quitting the head of the valley, a phenomenon due, Clem believes, to the acoustics of the high-walled valley, but now the noise seems to be growing louder and added to the disgruntled bellows is the thunder of beef on the run. The men are curious: the earlier gunfire had not caused a stampede so there seems little cause for one now.

Gus looks back up the valley but there is no sign of advancing cattle and that is when he realizes their mistake. He and Clem have been tricked by the darkness and strange acoustics. The cattle aren't coming down the valley, they are being driven up it. The thought is no sooner in his head than the first steers career around the tight bend and make a beeline for the spot where he and Clem now stand.

Acting instantly, they seek refuge at either side of the trail, each finding sanctuary behind boulders only seconds before the fifty strong bunch races past. Three men are driving them. They swing ropes and give voice to many cries of 'Yip', and 'Git along'.

In the dust of their passing Clem and Gus become reunited.

'Red Hammond,' says Gus.

'And Dusty Thoms and Rollo Wilson.'

'They'll come after us,' Gus prophesies. Without another word they begin to run along the valley.

Their horses are well rested and eager to run but the impediments of darkness and unfamiliar territory are a restriction on their pace. They are barely out of the valley, just beyond the pool where yesterday's gunfight occurred, when the sounds of pursuit carry on the still night air.

Looking over his shoulder, Clem shouts, 'I see only two.' They gallop on and although it is clear that their pursuers have seen them the intervening gap doesn't lessen.

'If they don't catch us before we get out of the hills,' Clem says, 'we should be able to beat them into town.'

Gus looks back, checks on the chasing pair. 'I don't think they're trying to catch us. They know these trails better than we do. Keep an eye on the skyline in case more of them are planning to cut us off.'

To test the purpose of their pursuers Clem and Gus spur extra effort from their mounts. Those behind increase their pace, too, just sufficient to maintain the gap between them, but now they add gunshots to the pursuit, firing their pistols as they ride.

'We're out of range,' declares Clem.

'Could be those shots are merely a signal, warning others that they need to make their play soon or we'll be out of reach.'

No sooner are the words spoken than Clem gives a shout. 'You're right, Gus. There's another two up on the ridge.'

Those riders are seen only briefly; in a moment they are gone from sight. Gus repeats his belief that the gunshots are a signal for them to descend and set up an ambush. More shots are fired by those behind and Gus returns them as a deterrent, although he is certain that those behind will not close the gap until the trap ahead has been sprung. Ahead, the trail twists left then right as it winds around jagged outcrops and for several moments they are hidden from the sight of those behind. Since that one brief sighting those riding the ridge have not been seen again but Gus suspects that already they are descending and waiting for him and Clem to ride into their waiting guns.

Suddenly Gus raises his left hand, an order to halt and pulls hard on the reins. Clem obeys one command and his mount the other, sagging back on its haunches until it is almost sitting on the ground.

'Follow me,' he tells his puzzled younger companion, and leads the way off the trail to seek refuge behind some high boulders. With their hands covering their horses' muzzles they wait silently and still for those in their wake.

They wait less than a minute, then the two riders, galloping hard in their anxiety to regain sight of their quarry, race past without a glance either to right or left. When they have navigated the next twist in the trail and ridden off into the night, Gus and Clem emerge from their sanctuary and follow. They travel cautiously, without haste, listening for activity ahead and watchful for another haven in which to hide when the rustlers return.

Up ahead, a series of gunshots crack the still night. Clem and Gus exchange grins as panic-filled shouts carry to them. The shooting ceases, but for the moment they have no way of knowing what injuries have been sustained.

'They'll come looking for us,' says Clem.

'They know they haven't much chance of finding us,' Gus tells him. 'I expect they'll be keener to get back to the valley and move the stolen cattle.'

Gus's hunch is right. From deep shadows they observe the returning rustlers. The four ride by in watchful fashion, in hope that they will discover the position of their quarry but suspecting that they are long gone over the hills to Enterprise.

Only Clem rides on towards Enterprise. Gus agrees to take up a post by the pool where he'll be able to observe any movement of rustlers and cattle. When Clem returns with Sheriff Bright Gus will be able to indicate the direction they have taken.

CHAPTER THIRTEEN

The sky is cloudless and the moon is bright as Clem clears the last ridge that leads down to Enterprise. He checks the stars and because the Big Dipper is still higher than the North Star he calculates that it is not yet midnight. Even so, he expects little activity in the town. The townsfolk will be in their homes, the cowhands will have returned to the ranches of their employers and the homesteaders will be asleep in their shacks and sod houses, regaining their strength for the next day to dawn. Sheriff Tom Bright, he assumes, will have to be brought from his bed to hear his story.

But a surprise awaits Clem. As he enters Drover Street the boardwalk lanterns still burn. Horses are tethered to the rails outside the Prairie Paradise and the noise that spills out from that establishment broadcasts the fact that business for the day is not yet done. Tugging at the reins, he slows the foam-flecked grey to a walk and they proceed slowly along the street. The earlier events of the evening have set his senses on high alert and when he catches a movement to his right he turns swiftly in the saddle.

A voice, quiet and hoarse, like a bullfrog croaking through a silk scarf, calls to him.

'It's Josh. Josh Grant.'

Clem heads the grey over to the veranda where the man he'd carried from the burning building sits on a high cane chair. Josh Grant's face is etched with lines of worry. He coughs as though his lungs are still full of smoke and he holds a square of white cotton to his mouth as though anything that he expels needs to be caught and inspected.

'What's happening?' asks Clem.

'Cattlemen are celebrating. Sheriff Bright announced earlier that he'd come across no evidence to suggest that Pat Baker hadn't been involved in rustling.'

Clem grunts his dissatisfaction.

Josh speaks again. 'He made some political noises to suggest that if he'd found any impropriety in the actions of Nat Erdlatter he'd be ordering a trial to get the matter sorted out, but as far as he could tell the established law of the range had been applied. All the eye-witnesses, he said, had been in agreement. He tried to pacify Jim Welsh and Harv Golden by agreeing that Erdlatter had no right to elect himself as arbiter, but Pat Baker had been caught red-handed in the act of over-branding cattle on Circle-E range. Every court in the land would have convicted him and sentenced him to hang.'

'Perhaps what I have to tell him will change his views,' says Clem.

At that moment the door behind Josh Grant opens. His daughter Lucy steps out. She pulls a shawl tightly around her shoulders and smiles at Clem.

'I heard voices,' she explains and rests a hand on her father's shoulder. 'Come inside,' she tells him, then to Clem adds, 'They say there's going to be trouble, that Jim Welsh is seeking a showdown with the cattlemen.'

As if on cue, from further along the street a mob emerges from one of the alleyways that lead through to Hill Street. Some carry lanterns, others burning brands. There is little in the way of noise to announce their march but judging by the way that men tumble out of the Prairie Paradise it is evident that their approach has been expected and reported by a lookout.

While they are some yards distant, two men step forward from among those who have left the Prairie Paradise and wait in the middle of the road. One man has a shotgun cradled in his arms; it is he who speaks first.

'Men, this demonstration of force doesn't help your cause. Mr Erdlatter acted in accord with accepted protocol. Rustlers are hanged. Pat Baker was caught in the act and suffered the penalty for his deed. Now clear the street. Go home. The matter is closed.'

A man steps out of the mob. 'You are supposed to represent the law, Tom Bright,' he says, 'but you just bend to the will of the cattlemen.'

'When I let you out of the cells earlier, Jim Welsh, I told you to go home. If you don't leave now you'll be back inside and the charge will be assaulting a law officer with a deadly weapon. They'll put you in state prison for a long time. Now go home.'

For several moments there is silence while both sides consider the probable outcome if someone doesn't back down. Clem Rawlings touches his horse's flanks with his spurs and moves forward. Behind him he hears the worried voice of Lucy Grant.

'Be careful, Clem.'

Clem rides his horse to a point between the two groups of men and stops.

'I'm Clem Rawlings,' he tells Tom Bright. 'Gus Farley and I were present when Pat Baker was hanged. You haven't heard our testimony.'

'I know that you weren't present when Pat Baker was caught,' the sheriff tells him, 'so there is nothing you can say that will contradict the testimony of the eye-witnesses.'

'You're wrong, Sheriff. I can prove that Pat Baker had nothing to do with cattle-rustling.'

Tyro Brooks, who is standing shoulder to shoulder with Sheriff Bright, speaks.

'Everyone knows that cattle have been stolen, Clem.'

'I'm not denying that, Marshal. The Tumbling-Y has lost stock as well as the Circle-E and probably other ranches too, but Pat Baker wasn't involved.'

'Don't listen to him, Sheriff.' This is Vinny Erdlatter, pushing his way to the forefront of the cattlemen who are ranged along the boardwalk in front of the Prairie Paradise. He is unsteady on his feet and his face wears an alcohol-induced flush that is apparent even in the dim light of the street lanterns. 'He can tell you nothing. Wasn't man enough to do what had to be done at the time and isn't man enough to live with it now.'

There are mutterings among the watchers of both sides, all wondering how Clem will react to this slur on his charcter.

Clem lets his eyes roam over the cowboys on the boardwalk. 'There seems to be a shortage of Circle-E riders, Vinny,' he says. 'Do you know where Red and his crew are right now?'

'Of course I do. They're back at the ranch.'

'You're wrong. They are nursing a herd of cattle in the hills. Stolen cattle, the cattle they accused Pat Baker of stealing.'

'Bah!' scoffs Vinny, looking at the faces of the nearest men, expecting to see other expressions of ridicule for Clem and support for himself.

'I've seen them, Sheriff,' Clem tells Tom Bright. 'Gus Farley is still there, watching them in case they decide to move the herd. If you organize a posse we'll be able to apprehend them. Red Hammond is the leader and has been using some of the Circle-E riders to amass a small herd which he expects to sell to a buyer from Buffalo.'

'That's crazy talk,' shouts Vinny, more anxious now because the gathered men seem to be listening to Clem.

'They duped you, Vinny,' says Clem. 'You and your father, too. Not only have they stolen your cattle but they got you to hang an innocent man to cover up their deeds.'

'That's a lie,' shouts Vinny, but his tone carries less conviction.

Tom Bright speaks, his words reflecting his unwillingness to accept any implication that his earlier decision regarding the guilt of Pat Baker is incorrect.

'What I want is for every man to get off the street. Go home. I'll decide in the morning if a posse is to be assembled.' He glares at Clem, making it clear that he will need more cause than his accusations before he'll go chasing shadows in the hills.

'We've got to go now,' urges Clem, then, getting little encouragement from the sheriff's expression, he makes his appeal to those gathered around. 'Every man here has a stake in this territory,' he declares, 'and when this incident is over you all have to live here. Grab the opportunity to resolve this matter together and hope that it will mean greater tolerance of each other in the future.'

He confronts those on the boardwalk, 'If you want to recover your stolen stock then come with me – and you,' he adds as he swings in the saddle to face the homesteaders, 'can prove the innocence of Pat Baker by capturing the real rustlers and proving that they are the very people who accused him and caused his death.'

At first his words are greeted with silence. Then slowly, one by one, murmurs of agreement can be heard. Slippy Anderson is the first volunteer to join and after him, from the other side of the street, Harv Golden speaks up.

'I'll ride with you,' he tells Clem, then nudges Jim Welsh to do likewise.

Jim has more to say; his eyes are fixed on Tom Bright. 'If Red Hammond is the ringleader then your days as sheriff are over. We don't need you to ride with us, we need a sheriff who upholds the law for cattlemen, farmers and townsfolk alike.'

'You need the law with you,' says Tyro Brooks, 'I'll saddle up.'

Thirty minutes later fifteen men: cattlemen, homesteaders and lawmen, ride out of Enterprise for the high country. They are led by Clem Rawlings but Sheriff Tom Bright, anxious to bolster the respect for the law, which is dramatically flagging in this territory, rides at his side. Vinny Erdlatter, too, is with them, convinced by Clem that he needs to be present when the rustlers are unmasked and the over-branded Circle-E steers are identified.

'They've been gone about two hours,' Gus reports when the posse reaches him. 'Pushing the herd hard like they are in a hurry to get somewhere – or think the Devil's hot on their heels.'

'How many?' asks Tyro Brooks.

'Cows? Upwards of four hundred. Tiny Duggett and a couple of drovers arrived with another bunch.'

'And men?'

'Eight.'

'Which way did they go?' asks Sheriff Bright, trying to establish some sort of authority within the group.

'I followed them east a while,' says Gus, 'as though they were heading for Buffalo but after a while they cut south.'

'We should give the horses a short rest,' says Tyro. 'No matter how hard the rustlers work they won't be able to make much headway in this terrain.'

The cowmen among the group acknowledge the marshal's common sense and the posse waits ten minutes, letting the horses drink from the pool.

It is barely daybreak when they hear the first calls of the drovers, perhaps half a mile away. Gus and Slippy Anderson scout ahead and report that the herd is stretched out, because the ravines and dips of the hills dictate that progress can only be achieved in single file.

'There's a stream up ahead,' Slippy informs everyone. 'They'll probably congregate there, let the critters drink while they have the opportunity; then, with daylight and low land approaching they'll try for a better pace.'

'Then that's where we'll take them,' states Tom Bright. 'By the river. We'll come down on them fast.'

Clem offers a suggestion: 'Send some men ahead,' he says. 'If they circle the herd and cross the stream they'll cut off any rustlers who try to escape that way.'

It is deemed a good plan and a five-man detachment, which includes Harv Golden and Jim Welsh and is led by Tyro Brooks, makes its way through the lingering darkness to lay the trap. The remainder of the posse divides into two groups, intending to attack in a pincerlike movement thirty minutes later.

It is Clem's hope that the rustlers will not have anticipated a posse leaving Enterprise before daybreak and that this surprise attack will cause them to surrender without a fight. It is not the prospect of danger to himself that promotes this hope but a desire for the rustlers to be captured so that the events that led to the hanging of Pat Baker can be revealed. But he is to be disappointed.

In the dim light, as the rustlers gather the cattle on the bank of the stream, they are as watchful as cavalry-men in hostile territory: the first indication of shifting shapes descending from the slopes brings a warning shout. The speed with which the new arrivals are approaching leaves them in no doubt that these men have come to take back the stolen cattle, but they count only five riders which, they figure, are not enough to outgun them. Before Tom Bright can announce his office and demand their surrender the rustlers are reaching for their weapons and throwing lead.

Tom Bright's men return gunfire. A rustler clutches at his chest and topples from his mount. The cattle begin to mill along the bank, running in all directions and splashing into the stream in an effort to escape the sudden outburst of noise.

A mixture of rifle and pistol shots fill the air as the two groups exchange fire over the backs of the steers. There is a yell of pain from a posse-man, who wheels away from the fray; he clings precariously to his saddle, determined not to fall to the ground where he might be trampled by the spooked cattle.

A bullet knocks Vinny Erdlatter's hat from his head and immediately he pulls his horse to a halt. He peers at those shooting at him and although there is still insufficient light to distinguish faces he is sure that the two of the shapes he can see belong to Tiny Duggett and Red Hammond. He wants to order them to cease fire, identify himself as the son of the man who pays their wages, but he knows how futile that will be. As the truth of the matter sinks home: that Clem Rawlings has spoken the truth and an innocent man has been hanged, his stomach lurches as though preparing to disgorge its contents.

For an instant, with only three of their attackers still advancing, the rustlers think they have won the fight. Confident of victory they ignore Tom Bright's demand to cease fire, and they continue firing in the lawman's direction. It is Carl Pelton who first sees the law rein-forcements approaching from the right. He yells a warning and some of the rustlers take up a position to resist the new threat.

With bullets flying around them as they join the fray, Clem and his group have little choice but to return fire. Their first fusillade lifts Dusty Thoms and Grat Todd out of their saddles, creating panic and confu-sion among the remaining five rustlers. Red Hammond urges them to keep fighting and when the hammer of his Colt strikes empty chambers he pulls his rifle from its scabbard and keeps a stream of lead flying over the heads of the fear-filled steers. But now his marksmanship is less effective, accuracy having been forsaken in the interest of continuous fire, which he hopes will deter the posse riders from closing in on their position.

With a shriek of pain a drover plunges from his horse; a spray of scarlet blood arcs through the air

150

towards Red. Instantly the man is lost from view under the hoofs of panic-filled cattle who, in wild-eyed frenzy, seek an escape route from the surrounding turmoil. Now, with only half the crew remaining, the former Circle-E foreman knows that there is nothing left but flight.

Turning his horse he heads towards the stream. He has a hunch that by the time the posse-riders manoeuvre a path through the crazed herd he will have enough of a head start to avoid capture. He kicks at his horse's flanks and urges it forward. His remaining allies, Tiny Duggett, Carl Pelton and Rollo Wilson, now low on ammunition, see his intention and decide to follow.

The posse's attack is becoming a bloodbath. Slippy Anderson has stopped a bullet although he is still in the saddle, and another of Clem's group is groaning and holding his stomach. Fearing that none of the rustlers will survive to give true testimony about the night that Pat Baker was killed, Clem gives chase to the fleeing outlaws. It is now easier to find a clear path among the scattering cattle and Clem is closing quickly on the rearmost rustler.

Just as they reach the edge of the stream the man turns and fires point blank at Clem but the gun is empty and he resorts to throwing it. Clem bends low and it flies harmlessly over his back. For a few strides they race neck and neck until Clem launches himself from the back of his animal and crashes into his adversary. Tiny Duggett is bigger and heavier than Clem but is still dislodged from his saddle and together they crash into the water.

For a big man Tiny is agile. He is first to his feet and growls as he recognizes his assailant.

'This time I'll kill you,' he tells Clem as he advances. He swings a great fist which, with difficulty, Clem avoids but in so doing stumbles and falls once more into the water. Tiny Duggett comes forward again, his hands reaching to grasp Clem's head and push him under the water.

Knowing he can't win against Tiny's strength, Clem moves quickly to avoid his clutches. Rising to his feet he scrambles backwards, deeper into the stream, barely staying upright as he treads on loose rocks beneath his feet. Tiny, moving forward and confident of his ability to hurt Clem, lurches at him again. His swinging right hand hits Clem in the chest, dumping him on his back, causing him to hit his head on hard rocks below the surface.

Shaking his head to clear away the effects of the blow, Clem sits in the water. Once more Tiny approaches and now a long, slim-bladed knife glints in his right hand while murder glows in his eyes. Clem's right hand has settled on a submerged rock. When he lifts his hand the rock comes free. As Tiny draws back his arm, Clem throws the rock. His aim is good. It hits Tiny between the eyes, dazing him and causing him to totter backwards.

The advance of the posse-men in pursuit of those rustlers fleeing across the river has increased panic among the cattle. They run in every direction, many are in the water which, at its deepest point, is no more than knee high. They are running, regardless of any obstacle that might hamper their route. Tiny Duggett staggers into the path of one beast. Lowering its head and twisting its neck it drives a long horn through Tiny's body.

Tiny screams, a dreadful sound which adds to the fright and rage of the crazed steer. It flings its head to free itself of the encumbrance; then, in its eagerness to escape the pandemonium behind, steps on Tiny, its sharp-edged hoofs bursting open the rustler's body, leaving him a bloody mass in its wake as it dashes to the far bank.

Clem stands over his enemy. There is nothing he can do except watch his last pain-filled moments. From the far bank comes the sound of more gunfire. The last of the rustlers have run into Tyro Brooks's trap. Clem hangs his head. No one is left to clear Pat Baker's name.

CHAPTER FOURTEEN

With his empty revolver back in its holster, Rollo Wilson follows Red Hammond and Carl Pelton up the far bank to the safety of the tree-lined slopes beyond. He is unconcerned by Tiny Duggett's struggle in the water because in reverse circumstances Tiny Duggett would have done nothing to help him. Rollo's only thought now is his own preservation and getting far from this territory in the shortest possible time. The appearance of Tyro Brooks' group of riders on the trail ahead shatters that scheme.

The marshal's demand for the fleeing rustlers to halt and throw down their weapons is only obeyed by Rollo. Knowing that he no longer has the means to resist arrest he pulls his horse to a halt and hoists his hands high in the air.

The reaction of Red Hammond and Carl Pelton is different. Their weapons are still hot in their hands and their instinct is to avoid capture. They jerk their horses' heads to the right, directing them towards denser cover while firing the last of the bullets. The answering volley from the posse-riders is lethal. Both men fall from their mounts and, in moments, lie dead on the ground.

The sight of Rollo Wilson among Tyro Brooks's band brings a grin of satisfaction to Clem's face. One survivor who, he believes, will stand trial and give an account of the events that led to Pat Baker's death. However, in answer to Sherff Bright's preliminary questions it becomes clear that Rollo and Dusty Thoms had been working a different part of the range that night and that Rollo's information is second hand.

Pat Baker, Rollo tells his captors, aware that rustlers were at work in the area, became suspicious when he saw a bunch of cattle being driven westwards. When he recognized the Circle-E riders Red Hammond knew that he couldn't allow him to escape. They hit upon the idea of putting the blame on him, hanging him as a rustler because they knew that Nat Erdlatter would condone the deed. Even when first Vinny and then Nat himself arrived they were confident enough to go through with their plan.

'Red knew the Erdlatters well enough to believe that they would accept his accusation of cattle rustling when it was pointed out that Pat worked for a homesteader. He was right. Those who were there that night couldn't stop laughing at how easily they'd fooled the old man.'

Vinny Erdlatter pales as he listens to this denunciation. His father's gullibility is matched by his own, both founded on biased views. He recalls the moment of superiority he'd known when his father had uttered *Get it done,* and he had whipped the pinto with his hat. That act had ended the life of an innocent man and now, as he examines the faces of those around him, he knows there will be a price to pay.

The two lawmen lead a string of horses with a body tied across the saddle back to Enterprise. They are accompanied by their one live prisoner, Clem, Gus, Vinny Erdlatter and the three wounded posse-men. The remainder of the posse, cowmen and farmers, drive the stolen cattle back to their home range, the camaraderie of a successful campaign providing common ground for the men to work together. Perhaps they are not yet friends but they talk as they chivvy steers and the first steps have been taken to a future where differences can be resolved without violence.

Two days later Agatha Grant reopens for business in temporary accommodation on Hill Street. Her husband and daughter are there to assist. There, as elsewhere in the town, the main topic of conversation is the fight in the hills and its aftermath. Respect for Nat Erdlatter has become a rare commodity, especially in the wake of Tom Bright's assertion that the cattle-baron and his son will be brought to trial.

'Hire a good lawyer,' the sheriff tells him. 'He'll convince a jury that Hammond was the driving force behind the lynching and if he'd still been alive he would be the one on trial for his life. But you did give the order and Vinny did act as executioner. There'll be punishment for both of you: a spell of imprisonment. I'd advise you to get your affairs sorted out in the next few days. Perhaps the Cattlemen's Association will take care of the ranch while you're away.'

The sheriff's advice to Erdlatter is all around town and although it meets with the approval of most people it is still unlikely to be enough to gain him re-election. Jim Welsh, much subdued since the defeat of the rustlers or, perhaps, consoled by Nat Erdlattrer's downfall, is still vociferous in his belief that another, more independent man is required for the office of county sheriff. But his arguments are now expressed with calm reasoning, thereby gaining the support of townspeople, cattlemen and homesteaders alike. The name of their town marshal Tyro Brooks is increasingly mentioned as the ideal candidate.

Tyro Brooks is as flattered by this new-found respect of the citizens as he is by the more personal interest that Lucy Grant has recently shown in him. This morning he is heading for her mother's eating-house as she steps outside to give parcels to two men who are making final adjustments to the saddle straps of their horses.

'Some bread and cheese,' she says, handing over a wrapped bundle, 'and there are some apples in the bag.'

Clem puts them in his saddle-bag, which is already bulging with his change of clothing.

'You'll let us know where you settle, won't you?'

'You'll get a letter within the month,' Clem promises.

'And you'll be sure to visit if you come back this way?'

'Can't wait to see the rebuilt premises. It'll be an eating-house to be proud of,' says Gus.

The look Clem throws in his direction is one of reprimand. He knows Gus has no intention of coming back to Enterprise; it is his creed never to return to a place he has left behind. As he loosens the rein of his horse from the hitching pole Lucy steps forward and catches his arm.

'You'll always be welcome here,' she says and swiftly embraces him. She steps back on to the boardwalk and is joined by Tyro Brooks.

A buggy draws to a halt in the street. Sepp Yates calls a greeting to Clem and Gus, his daughter is at his side. The cowboys approach the vehicle, Gus walking around the horses to stand beside Sepp, while Clem stays at the nearside. Joanna's expression is cold as she looks from Clem to the sidewalk where Lucy Grant is returning to the eating-house.

'We wondered why you hadn't been back to the ranch,' she says, 'but I guess now the reason is obvious.'

Clem follows her gaze but says nothing.

'We intended to make the Tumbling-Y our first stop this morning,' says Gus. 'On our way to say goodbye.'

'Goodbye?' Joanna can't hide her surprise. She examines Clem's face with wide, worried eyes.

'We've been heading for Montana ever since we quit the Circle-E,' he explains, 'It's taken us a while to get started but now we're on our way.'

'Oh!' she exclaims. 'After all that has happened I

thought you'd stay here.'

Her father speaks in agreement. 'Place is about to change,' he says, 'we need good people like you two to help it grow.'

'We're just cattle-pushers,' says Clem.

'We need cattle-pushers, don't we, Pa?' Her words are rushed and carry a hint of panic.

'Why sure,' says Sepp. 'There's always work at the Tumbling-Y.'

'Guess we just want to see a bit more country,' Clem tells them.

Sepp gives a grunt of amusement. 'Seems to be the way it's been since the Pilgrim Fathers landed here, young men pushing on to pastures new.'

'Long time since I was called a young man,' says Gus, and he and Sepp laugh.

Joanna and Clem gaze at each other, her eyes are damp and he pretends not to notice.

'Well, good luck to you,' says Sepp Yates, then slaps the rump of his horses with the long leathers.

The buggy barely travels two wheel turns before Joanna tells her father to halt.

'Clem,' she calls, and he follows until once more he's alongside her. 'I just wanted to say thank you for what you did for Pat.'

Clem removes his hat and wipes his forearm across his brow although the day is not yet so warm that sweat could have formed there. 'It wasn't enough,' he says.

Joanna bows her head, being contrite, although the words, when they come, are not as difficult for her to say as she expects.

'What I've learned,' she tells him, 'is that in the circumstances I believe it was as much as any man could have done and certainly more than anyone else did.'

Although her words are spoken with a quiet earnestness, Clem detects a renewed warmth in her tone. 'I appreciate that,' he tells her.

For a moment they look at each in silence. Slowly and gently a smile brightens her face and after a moment he returns it.

'If you come back this way you will look us up, won't you?' she says.

He nods, then Sepp flicks the reins and, rattling over deep, dry ruts, the buggy continues its journey along Hill Street.